THE WATCHERS of SPACE

Nancy Etchemendy

AN AVON CAMELOT BOOK

For
Billy and Margo

With special thanks to
Mr. Howell and his fifth grade class of 1975–76,
Alice Maxwell School,
Sparks, Nevada

THE WATCHERS OF SPACE is an original publication of
Avon Books. This work has never before appeared in book
form.

AVON BOOKS
A division of
The Hearst Corporation
1790 Broadway
New York, New York 10019

First Camelot Printing, April 1980

CAMELOT TRADEMARK REG. U. S. PAT. OFF. AND IN
OTHER COUNTRIES, MARCA REGISTRADA, HECHO EN
U. S. A.

Printed in the U. S. A.

OP 10 9 8 7 6 5 4 3

TABLE OF CONTENTS

Chapter One

The Golden Man

William lurched backward, grunting in pain as he rammed into a tree. It was a pine. He felt its rough bark through his coveralls and smelled the strong fragrance of its pitch. For a bottomless moment he stood in a kind of startled daze, his hands clapped tightly over his ears. Every tree and bush echoed with the shrieking whistle that was only too familiar to him. It was the sound of air escaping through another hole in the spaceship's outer wall. The metal bugs were at it again.

"Maggie!" he shouted. "Maggie, where are you?"

He had left her nearby at the edge of the pond. She often spent hours there watching the fish as they glided along through the clear, shallow water. He took several unsteady steps forward, pulling his hands away from his ears in case she answered. Waves of sound shook his body. He had never heard the whistle so loud before.

"Maggie!" he cried again.

"Here!" He heard her, faintly, from among the distant trees. Dimly he saw the glint of her bright coveralls as she hurried toward him. "Another hole?" she shouted as she stopped beside him, her eyes squeezed half-shut with fear and pain.

He nodded, then grabbed her arm and pulled her toward the hatch. "Let's get out of here before the air pressure drops," he yelled.

"But the animals! The trees! They'll all be killed," she cried, jerking stubbornly away from him. "Shouldn't we try to help or something?"

William knew she was right. If the ship's engineers didn't make it in time, the living things in the Earth chamber would soon perish. But at the same time, he knew that Maggie's safety was more important than the lives of any of the animals.

"Go on! Let's get out of here," he shouted. "There's nothing we can do."

Swiftly, he opened the hatch and pushed Maggie through it, then climbed out after her. For a moment, he wanted to leave it unsealed so that life-giving air could get through to the chamber. But that moment passed and he knew what he had to do. Savagely he turned the handwheel; there was an abrupt silence.

He slid to the floor, leaning his back against the cold metal of the hatch. There was no sound in the cool light of the corridor, for the thick, orange carpet muffled footsteps and voices alike.

"Maggie, are you all right?" he whispered.

She knelt on the floor, her forehead pressed tightly against the wall. He heard her swallow a sob. "Yes, I think so," she answered.

William squeezed his eyes shut so tightly that he saw colored sparkles in the darkness. How silly he had been, hoping that the Earth chamber would be spared.

The sudden weight of a warm hand on his shoulder startled him. He opened his eyes and found himself staring at the chief engineer's faintly shiny, whiskerless chin.

"Up you get, William," said the young man, lifting him to his feet. "You and your sister get away from here. We're going to crack that hatch, and it won't be pleasant."

"You're here already!" cried William excitedly. "You've got to hurry. All the animals . . ."

The engineer grinned a soft grin that seemed to hide a trace of gloom. "We'll take care of it. Go on," he said. But he caught the edge of William's sleeve and added, "Say, thanks for sealing off the chamber. It was the right thing to do."

William shook his head. "Oh, that's okay," he said quickly, hoping the engineer would not notice his red cheeks. He turned toward Maggie. "Come on. We'd better go."

They fled down the corridor in tense silence until the distant sound of rushing air stopped them. "That's it," murmured William, gazing back toward the Earth chamber. "They've cracked the hatch. I sure hope they made it in time."

Maggie nodded, the corners of her mouth drooping with sadness. She turned and trudged off down the long hall without a word.

"What's wrong?" asked William, when he had caught up with her.

She stared down at her feet, but he saw the glint of a tear as it rolled off her cheek. "I'm scared," she whispered. "We're going to die, aren't we?"

Maggie was usually so brave that William was not used to seeing her cry. It gave him a dark, empty feeling inside. "Hey, don't worry," he said, handing her his handkerchief. "There's a way out for the Genesis. We just have to find it, that's all."

"There's no way out," she said fiercely, rubbing her red eyes. "It was a silly dream all along. I've always thought so. Now here we are, stuck between stars with no hope."

"Oh, come on!" chided William softly. "You don't want to believe that."

She handed the rumpled handkerchief back to him. "Sorry I cried," she said. "I didn't mean to."

"It's okay," he answered, slipping his arm through hers. "I'm still proud of you. Not many guys have a little sister as brave as you."

"I don't feel very brave right now," she said. Her smile was a weak one.

"Of course you don't. Neither do I," he answered. "But we can't just give up. We have to remember, this ship has been in space for hundreds of years. There've been problems before, but we've always solved them, and we can solve this one, too. We have to believe that."

"But it's hard, William." Her voice was tight and trembling. "There are more holes every day. It's getting to the point where they can hardly keep up the repairs. I'm not deaf. I've heard the talk. They say the Genesis is a doomed ship."

William could think of no answer. He, too, had heard talk. Perhaps Maggie was right. Perhaps it was all a silly dream from the start. Human beings didn't belong in space, out here in the blackness where the only divider between them and death was a flimsy metal wall. They belonged on a planet, yet it would take hundreds of years to reach the nearest one.

He felt as if there were two wrestlers struggling inside him. Half of him cried out in pain that it was unfair, that he should have been born on a planet that rode peacefully about a warm sun. Half of him hated space and the death it stood for. But the other half of him knew that space was in his bones, that space, no matter how harsh it seemed, was his birthplace. He loved its stark beauty. But he also knew that it was strong, sometimes too strong.

"Maybe they say the Genesis is doomed. Well, that's because they've given up," he said to Maggie. "But *I* haven't given up, and I won't."

They walked on for some time without speaking. Behind them, William could still hear the clamor of the engineers as they fought to repair the puncture in the Earth chamber. He found himself thinking anxiously of the falcons again.

Smiling wistfully, he looked down at the long, red scar on the back of his right hand. He remembered the day the falcon had clawed him. It had frightened him, and he refused to go back to the chamber again for weeks afterward. Yet, after a time, he'd gotten over his fear. The falcons were his favorite animals now, and he was worried about them.

"William," said Maggie quietly as they walked, "I have an idea."

"What?" he asked.

"Will you come with me up to the observation cone? Right away? I—I don't want to stay around here."

William looked at her, a little puzzled. "The observation cone? Are you sure? I mean . . ."

"It's quiet there," she answered. "I just need to think, and I don't really mind the stars, you know."

William nodded. "You're crazy," he said, grinning. "But—okay. Let's take the stairs."

"Thanks," said Maggie, suddenly beaming. "Hey! Last one there's a rotten egg!" And, without warning, she rushed off ahead of him.

William followed more slowly. His heart was not really in the race.

5

He loved the Earth chamber. Compared to it, the rest of the huge ship seemed cold and lifeless. In the Earth chamber, shadows were sharp and the air was alive with the sights and smells of plants and animals. It was just the way he imagined a planet would be. There was dark, moist soil that felt good on bare toes; there were ponds full of fish; there were birds, and all kinds of trees—some with huge, green leaves. Sometimes when he was there he could almost forget that if all went well, his great-grandchildren would be old, old men by the time the Genesis came near to a real planet again. Sometimes the chamber seemed almost to be a little planet in itself, separate from the ship.

But today had brought an end to all those daydreams. The Earth chamber had walls, too—walls that could get holes in them.

"Come on!" called Maggie as she reached the stairway hatch and flung it open.

"I'm coming," he answered, running to catch up. Breathing hard, he burst through the small doorway and looked straight up. The spiral staircase appeared to go upward for kilometers until it ended in a small spot of dim light far above. Running down the center of the stairwell on thick cables and steel beams was a small, windowless elevator which even now was on its way up at breathtaking speed. But William always liked the solitude of the softly lit staircase better than the grinding, crowded elevator.

"Hurry up, slowpoke," called Maggie from somewhere above. Her voice echoed hollowly down to him.

He began the long climb. It was always hardest at first. But he knew that, because of the way the ship was designed, the artificial gravity would become weaker and weaker as he approached the top of the staircase. William often thought the Genesis looked much like the barbells that he had seen weightlifters straining with in the ship's gym. The ship had two great, spoked wheels and a long, slender tube—the main hold—running from the center of one wheel to the center of the other. And the entire ship spun around this tube, as if some cosmic weightlifter had started it rolling down an invisible hill. The spinning made it feel as if there was normal Earth gravity in the rims of the wheels. But nearer the center of the wheels the spinning had less of an effect, until finally, in the main hold, no gravity could be felt at all. Inside the spokes of each wheel were located the long, spiral stairways. As William climbed up the spoke, away from the wheel rim and toward the ship's center, he weighed less and less.

He could see Maggie, far above him, bounding up the steps three and four at a time in the low gravity. "Wait for me!" he called, beginning to feel better.

He had always enjoyed climbing the stairs. It filled him with a warm glow and cleared his mind. He could think better as his strong legs carried him upward.

Every day there were more and more hull punctures. At this rate, the great starship would never reach the end of its amazing journey between the stars. Someday, very soon, there would not be enough air left inside the Genesis to support life.

He knew what the problem was; if only he could help solve it. Several years ago (it seemed centuries), the Genesis had passed through an ordinary cloud of deep-space hydrogen. No one had thought much about it at the time. But later, it was discovered that the ship had picked up billions of tiny creatures while going through the cloud. They needed no air to survive. The little creatures would not have made any trouble for the starship if it hadn't been for one thing. They liked to eat metal. And to make matters even worse, the ship's scientists and technicians, working constantly all this time, had been unable to find a way of killing them.

William stopped a moment to catch his breath. Leaning over the railing he looked far down to the murky bottom of the stairwell. The Genesis was slowly being eaten away by tiny, living creatures even smaller than one cell of William's own skin. The colonists named them "metal bugs," creatures that had evolved in the black, airless depths of space. There was nothing they could do about it. The starship and all the space pioneers aboard her were doomed—doomed to die between stars, hundreds of years away from home and hundreds of years away from the closest inhabitable planet. The ship would never reach her destination, and neither would the men, women, and children inside her. They would all die unless they could either find a way to kill the creatures, or somehow reach a planet.

From far above, William heard Maggie's distant laughter tumbling down like the magic conversation of two neighboring suns. She had reached the top; William imagined her smiling with delight in the weightlessness of the main hold. He knew she enjoyed the feathery freedom of zero-gravity more than anything else. She could forget her fears in the joy of free-fall. He turned and bounded up the stairs after her.

Maggie was in the observation cone waiting for him when he got there. He hesitated outside the hatch. The stars meant many things to him now—terror and beauty, all at once. He needed a moment to get ready for them.

"William, come in. It's lovely," he heard Maggie call.

Taking a deep breath, he went inside and closed the hatch behind him.

At once the immense panorama of space hit him. Dim, eerie light from the billions of stars seeped through the huge, plastic dome that formed the nose of the ship. He could not speak. It was always the same, always as if he had never seen space before. He allowed himself to float easily in the center of the chamber, taking time to enjoy the sudden feeling of separation. He and the motionless stars were one in the darkness, while the Genesis wheeled freely around him as if on a course of its own.

It was musty in the chamber. In a back corner of his mind, William sensed that no fresh, fragrant air came through the ventilators in this room. The little coils designed to suck unneeded water from the air were silent here. He remembered a time when there were soft, creamy lights in the observation cone. Once, the colonists had met on Sundays in this chamber to give thanks for their good fortune. But that was long ago. Few of those aboard the Genesis liked looking at the stars anymore. To most, they meant only death.

What a strange and wonderful dream it all was. He almost wanted to laugh. It was a peculiar thought—a space voyage lasting more than a thousand years, a long and lonely journey from Earth to the nearest star with planets, a search for a better life, a better way. A new start for mankind—that's what his history book said. But look at the great dream now.

"Aren't they pretty?" Maggie broke the silence.

"Yes, and scary, too," answered William, making his way toward her.

"I can't believe it's happening," she said, half whispering. "It's like the world is ending."

"Yes." He shivered at the thought. "That's how it seems."

Maggie laughed softly. "Maybe if we make a wish, and we wish very hard..."

"I read in a book that people used to wish on stars," chuckled William, dryly. "We have plenty of those."

"We certainly do," she replied.

William chose a large, bright star and closed his eyes. "I wish everything would turn out fine," he thought.

Suddenly he felt Maggie grab his arm. "William, what was that?" she hissed. There was surprise and even a tinge of horror in her voice.

William opened his eyes. "What was what?"

"You didn't see it?" she replied. "There was something out there!"

He looked out through the clear dome. The view was the same as always—the black velvet of space dotted with the hard, round lights of distant suns. "Are you sure? I don't see anything," he said. But Maggie's excitement had infected him and his heart beat fast. Perhaps she had seen nothing special—a wandering asteroid or a gas cloud. But on the other hand . . . "Maybe you imagined it," he said.

"No," she insisted. "I saw something. It was like a—I don't know. It was huge and shiny."

William felt excitement rushing through his body like electricity. Maggie's face was pale in the starlight. Her eyes were wide and steady. He knew she wasn't lying. She *had* seen something, and judging from the way she looked, it was nothing ordinary.

The roar of his own swiftly flowing blood filled his ears as he let himself drift toward the dome. "The thing you saw—did it move?" he whispered.

"Of course it did. It moved away from the dome, didn't it?" There was a sharp edge of impatience in her voice.

"I mean . . . " William fumbled with the words. "Was it alive?"

She shook her head. "I don't know. I've never seen anything like it before."

He crouched in the darkness where the plastic of the dome joined the metal of the Genesis' hull. He peered out

10

into space, half afraid of what he might see, but also afraid of what he might miss. His eyes burned.

It seemed as if they huddled, watching for hours, before Maggie exclaimed, "Look! There it is again!" She pointed a small finger.

William drew his breath in sharply. Outside the observation cone drifted a *huge, golden man*! He was at least four times as tall as any other man William had ever seen, and every particle of his gigantic body seemed to glow with an eerie, yellow light. He wore no space suit—only a short, loosely fitting tunic gathered at the waist with a wide, gold belt. His great feet were encased in heavy sandals with straps that climbed from his ankles, up his thick calves, to his knees. His golden hair was held by an engraved band that shone like a thousand stars. But most awesome of all was the marvelous shining bow which he held easily in one strong hand, and the quiver which hung on his back, filled with arrows the size of spears.

William forgot to breathe. The great, glowing man was slowly and deliberately beckoning him forward, inviting him out into the awful emptiness of space.

Chapter Two

Trapped

"He wants me to go out there!" William leaned forward in excitement. He could hardly believe his eyes. "This is crazy," he whispered.

"No it's not," said Maggie, crouched beside him. "He's real. I *know* it."

"Yes, he's real," answered William. "There's no doubt of that. But what does he want? Why doesn't he go up to the bridge viewers and get the captain's attention?"

"I don't know," Maggie replied. "Funny, isn't it?"

"Yes," he said, drifting as close to the dome as he could. When his nose was almost pressed against the plastic, he looked straight into the giant's face and pointed back toward the bridge. "Bridge. Go to the bridge," he said, mouthing the words carefully.

To William's astonishment, the giant's answer was quick and sure. Shaking his huge, golden head, he clearly mouthed the word no, and pointed first at William, then at himself.

"Omigosh!" cried Maggie. "This *is* crazy. He understands you. I think he speaks English."

William pushed away from the dome and floated backward toward the center of the chamber. "I don't believe this," he whispered. "How in the world can he speak English? How can he breathe out there? How did he get there in the first place?"

For a moment, neither of them spoke. William gazed through the dome in confusion and amazement; the giant continued to beckon, smiling warmly all the while.

Maggie drifted up beside him and said in a low voice, "I guess you'll never know the answers to those questions unless . . ."

"Unless I go outside and find out what he wants." William finished the sentence for her. He clenched his jaw, partly to keep it from trembling. Excitement was building up inside him. He felt almost ready to explode. "And that's what I intend to do," he said.

"Take me with you," hissed Maggie, grabbing his arm.

He looked over at her in surprise. "Maggie, it's going to be very dangerous," he replied.

"What does *that* matter? Don't you see, William? What if he can help us somehow?" Her eyes were aglow with a curious fire that William had seldom seen there.

"Yes, I've thought of that," he answered slowly. "On the other hand, what if he wants to kill us? That's just as likely."

"I don't care if he kills us." She sounded almost fierce. "If *he* doesn't do it, the metal bugs will."

"Listen, Maggie, you're right and we both know it. The Genesis is a dead ship unless we find a way out of this mess. I don't know for sure. I can only guess, but that fellow out there may be our key to life for this ship. There's a lot at stake here, and since he won't talk to the captain, it's up to us to do our best to find out what's going on."

"I know that," she said, impatiently. "Just let me go with you."

"No," he said, flatly.

Maggie looked as if he'd slapped her in the face. "Why not?" she demanded. "Don't give me any of that stuff about being too little. I could help, and you know it."

"Look, don't think I'm trying to be a hero. I could use some company out there, you know. It's just that I'll never get out of the ship without being discovered unless you help me from inside. Don't forget that panel of lights on the bridge. It'll come on like a Christmas tree the second I open the airlock," he said, straining to keep his voice down.

"But there's nothing I can do about that even if I stay behind," said Maggie.

"But there *is* something you can do—something that will make the difference between success and failure for us."

Maggie narrowed her eyes and pressed her lips into a thin line. Her silence was filled with disappointment.

"Please, Maggie, please," said William, looking straight into her hard, blue eyes. "You know I'd rather take you with me, but I'll never make it through the hatch unless you help from inside."

She turned to look once again at the huge, glowing figure beyond the dome. Then she answered slowly, "All right, then. What do I have to do?"

William sailed without a sound down the dimly lit central corridor of the main hold. Occasionally he pushed against the curved wall for added speed. He didn't have much time, and he didn't want to risk missing the giant by being too slow.

He met no one as he rushed past storage areas and deserted maintenance rooms, until at last he came to the hatch that led to the ferry hangar. Quickly, he opened the metal door and clambered through it into a gigantic chamber. He paused for a moment, staring into the shadowy distance, listening hard for some sign of life. But he heard only his own shallow breathing; no shadows moved. He was alone in the half-darkness, with the twenty-five empty ferry boats that lay in their cradles waiting for a day that might never come. It seemed that long ago he had come here often, always alone, to play a secret game that he had invented—a game in which he was the hero who piloted the first ferry to the surface of the new planet—a game in which he was the first colonist to arrive on Earth II, leaving the Genesis drifting like an empty seed pod in space.

But he had no time for games now. He pushed off toward the deep shadows at the other end of the hangar where he knew there was a small airlock and a storage room for extravehicular equipment.

At the hatch of the storage room he hesitated, listening. He heard nothing but the distant rumble of the power generators far in the aft section. Grabbing the hatch, he ducked inside. There, neatly arranged along the walls, hung dozens of space suits of various sizes, each one complete and ready for use. William had often practiced suiting up in safety drills, though he had never actually been outside the starship. It took him only a few minutes to find the proper size, slip into it, and adjust it.

He glanced at his watch. He had only five minutes left to get into the airlock, depressurize it, and prepare for exit on Maggie's signal. Moving stiffly in the unfamiliar suit, William climbed out of the storage chamber and down into the lock, closing and sealing the hatch behind him.

He took a deep, shaky breath. This was it. He was alone in the elevator-size airlock, with only minutes to go before he would launch himself into empty space. He tried not to think about it, concentrating on the lever that controlled air pressure inside the tiny cubicle. More important than that, he could see the green all-clear light that would flash when Maggie gave the signal.

He could imagine Maggie, a kilometer away from him by now, peering through the viewport in the thick, sealed door of the bridge. He thought of the ship's officers at their posts, each performing a different task. There were helmsmen, navigators, communications officers, and laser operators, watching for stray meteors. He thought of Captain Stone, looking fine in his silver uniform, seated at the central panel. But there was only one man William really had to fear. That was the maintenance control officer who sat before a panel covered with hundreds of tiny lights. If anyone caught William, it would be that man. He would sound an immediate alarm when the red airlock light came on.

William checked his suit one last time and, satisfied, threw the evacuation lever. The air pressure inside the lock began to drop until at last everything outside his suit became silent and unreal in the vacuum. It was only the suit that kept him alive, only the suit that conducted sound, now. Breathlessly, he laid his hands on the gleaming wheel of the outer hatch. Staring at the green light, he waited.

Maggie should already have the wall intercom outside the bridge dialed for the airlock station where he waited. If so, all she had to do now was push one button and the green light would come on. He fidgeted with the handwheel. What was the officer doing now? Writing on a clipboard perhaps, bending over his panel? If only he would turn his head, or speak to another officer. If only something would distract him. The minutes seemed to creep by.

Then, suddenly, before his straining eyes, *the green*

light winked on! Now was his chance! One last time, he wished for luck, then twisted the handwheel on the outer hatch as hard and fast as he could. Soundlessly, the hatch fell away, swinging into the empty darkness outside the starship's hull. Knees shaking, William lowered himself through it and out onto the catwalk that ran alongside.

He felt cold and empty inside as he struggled to attach his safety line to the railing and slip his heavy metal shoes into the magnetic imprints on the hull. Only the magnets and the railing kept him from dropping away from the spinning Genesis and drifting helplessly off into space. The safety line was only a last resort if anything accidental should happen.

Swiftly he closed the hatch, praying that the maintenance control officer had not noticed anything. He stood up slowly, fighting to keep back the wall of terror that threatened him. He had never been outside before and the sight of the cold stars wheeling like a carousel before his eyes left him dizzy and frightened. He clutched at the handrail, not trusting the magnets that held him in place. He felt as if he were walking upside down on an unsteady overhang, above a bottomless pit. It turned his stomach to ice inside him.

Before and behind him the slender midsection of the Genesis stretched a kilometer in either direction, gleaming dully in the starlight. He could see the forward wheel, distant and tremendous, looming up in front of him and knew that if he turned around he would find a similar view of the aft wheel. Warm, yellow light poured from the viewports and filled him with a yearning to be back inside; but he fought it, remembering the golden man who softly smiled and beckoned from outside the observation cone.

Unsteadily, he switched on the headlamp built into the helmet of his suit and began to move down the catwalk.

Wherever his light shown, he saw with dismay that the metal of the ship was corroded and pock-marked, like the surface of a miniature moon. The tiny creatures from the gas cloud had been at work everywhere, slowly and relentlessly devouring the Genesis.

As he made his way gradually toward the nose of the ship, the mammoth forward wheel grew larger. Two of its gigantic spokes rose in front of him, reaching hundreds of meters out into space, ending in the rim of Wheel I. Inside, hundreds of people were going about their daily business, hardly aware of the dizzying rate at which they spun on their journey between the stars. He stopped to catch his breath and blink the sweat out of his eyes.

After a moment's rest, he began the trek again, lifting each leg slowly and setting it down firmly in the next imprint. But a few moments later, something stopped him in his tracks. He had a sudden, uncomfortable feeling that someone was standing behind him. He was about to turn around and look when a voice suddenly crackled over his helmet radio.

"Congratulations, my friend," it said. "Welcome to space."

He almost lost his balance as he turned and discovered the huge, golden man standing directly between him and the airlock hatch. *His retreat was blocked!*

Chapter Three

Orion and Starnight

Hundreds of thoughts poured through William's mind in the next few seconds. Most of all, he was sorry for ever having come outside at all. The giant's sheer size overwhelmed him, and in spite of all his hopes about the possibility of help, William began to wonder if he wouldn't be smarter to just turn his back and run. He soon realized, though, that it would be futile to run. There were no hiding places on the hull, and besides, his progress would have been too slow in the bulky space suit.

For a long moment, he and the giant stared at each other. Then, slowly, a grin spread over the giant's bearded face and he chuckled softly. "Do I frighten you, little lion?" he said. His voice, even through the tinny-sounding helmet radio, was as deep as the bass notes of a pipe organ.

William cleared his throat and tried to make his voice sound strong and firm. "Yes, as a matter of fact you do," he answered.

At that, the giant's grin broadened. "Yet here you are, in spite of everything," he said. Then, as if to himself, he added, "Yes, I think we chose well."

"I don't understand," said William. "What is this all about? Who are you, and what are you doing here? And how are you activating my radio?"

"Your radio?" asked the giant, his forehead creased in a frown.

"Yes," said William, "you know—how can I hear you?" And he pointed toward his helmet.

"Oh, that! The little hearing device," said the giant, smiling again. "I have my ways. The mind is a powerful tool." Then, stroking his beard contemplatively, he added, "But the details are better kept secret from a race like yours."

"A race like ours?" exclaimed William. "What's wrong with us?"

"Mmm—nothing perhaps," replied the giant. "We simply prefer not to take too many chances in the beginning."

William was completely at a loss. "Sir, you wanted me to come out here. You must have had a reason," he said after some hesitation.

"Yes," said the giant, "I had a very good reason. I have been chosen to give you a message, my friend."

Something in the giant's tone of voice made William shiver as he looked up into the great, shining face. "A message? But how could you have a message? I don't even know who you are or who sent you," he said in puzzlement. "This whole thing is crazy. Things like this just don't happen!" For a terrible moment he wondered if he were dreaming.

"Ah, but they *do* happen," said the giant, stooping to hold a hand out toward William. "Touch me. You will find that I am very real."

Cautiously, William touched the giant's huge, golden hand with the tip of one glove. He was not really surprised to find it firm. But wouldn't it feel firm, William wondered, even if he were dreaming? His thoughts were interrupted.

"And of course you deserve an explanation," the giant continued. "To begin with, shall I give you a name to call me?"

"That would be helpful," answered William, almost laughing at the strangeness of the question. Slowly his fear was leaving him and he was beginning to relax a little.

"Well, you may call me Orion. I am a member of the Brotherhood of Watchers. It is they who have sent me here to speak with you."

William frowned. "But I don't know anything about 'Watchers.' There must be some mistake. Perhaps you have the wrong person."

But Orion shook his great head solemnly. "No, my friend. There is no mistake. I have watched this ship many days now. I have watched every person aboard her. And I have chosen *you* above all the others to receive this message."

"Why me?" asked William, amazed. "If you've been watching us, you know there are hundreds of people aboard this ship who are stronger and smarter than I am."

Orion smiled and hooked his great thumbs into his belt. "I looked for a good, strong heart. I looked for one who would not doubt, who would have the courage to try unlikely paths. You—William Murdock—I looked for you."

William could not quite explain why those words made him suddenly begin to tremble. "Oh, my gosh," he said. "What have I gotten into?"

The giant laughed aloud, a warm and buttery sound that helped to still William's chattering teeth. "You have gotten into a chance to save this ship, my friend."

William clung dizzily to the handrail, trying to overcome his surprise. "You mean you're going to help us?" he cried.

"Perhaps," answered Orion, stroking his beard again. "But only after you have made us certain. Only after all our questions are answered. And only if you are willing to help, too."

"Of course we'll help! We'll do anything at all, anything—if we can just get rid of these metal bugs."

Orion looked down at him gravely and blinked. "Yes, I realize that. But the matter is not quite that simple. In the first place, it is beyond a Watcher's power to take life or to cause injury to any living thing. We are limited. We can guide you, and we can give you certain tools. But we cannot simply kill the creatures that plague your ship."

"What did you have in mind?" asked William slowly.

"There is a solution to your problem which you have perhaps not considered—transport the Genesis to her destination before it is too late."

William could not have been more startled if Orion had shot him with one of his spear-like arrows. "But—but that's impossible! We're hundreds of years away from Earth II. We can't travel any faster," he stammered.

Orion broke into a wide smile. His straight, golden teeth gleamed. "You are wrong," he replied. "It can be done. But you must be aware that the road to that goal is a long and dangerous one, filled with risks and uncertainties."

William's face had grown warm and damp inside his helmet. The sharp taste of his own perspiration filled his mouth. "I expected that," he said, licking his lips. "But then, I suppose it would be worth it even if I had to die . . ."

"Perhaps it will not come to that. But I wanted you to

understand," answered Orion. With that, he reached deep into the folds of his tunic, into some hidden pocket or pouch, and drew forth a magnificent sword and a leather sheath.

William whistled softly as he stared at the sword's gilt handle and blade which were covered with strange symbols and pictures. "I've never seen anything so beautiful in all my life," he whispered. The sword pulsed white and orange against the darkness of space.

"This is the sword Starnight. If you choose to try your hand at saving your people, this will be your first tool."

Something about the beauty of the weapon filled William with new courage and determination; he answered without hesitating. "There is no question. All I want is a chance to try."

"Just as I had hoped," replied the giant. There was a strange light in his eyes that seemed to make them shine even more than usual. "If you can solve the puzzle of Starnight, the sword can lead you to a place where you will find gleaming stones. These stones can be used to transport your ship anywhere in this galaxy within mere seconds."

"Oh my gosh," murmured William. "There really *is* a way, then."

"Indeed there is," replied Orion softly. He placed the sword and its sheath in William's trembling hands. "But you can be sure I am telling you the truth when I say that there is great evil in this world, evil which sees you and knows of your presence here. Don't think it will be easy. You must have a strong heart."

As William looked on, Orion's eyes shone brighter and brighter until at last they seemed like two gleaming beacons set into his face. Slowly, his heavy, sandaled feet drifted away from the Genesis' hull.

"But—wait a minute!" cried William, as he realized that the giant was leaving. "Won't you explain? I don't understand. Tell me how to use the sword."

But Orion was already meters away from the ship. "I can say no more, friend," he called. "All will be clear to you in time, if I have judged you right—if you can pass the test. In the meantime, take heed. Never falter in your purpose."

Before William had time to say anything else, the giant bolted away like an arrow loosed from a heavenly bow. His golden body shrank in seconds to a dot of twinkling light, then faded altogether. William was alone again on the bleak skin of the Genesis.

In wonder, William looked down at the sword. He could only guess how much it would weigh in the normal gravity of the ship's wheel. But it felt good in his hands. It was superbly crafted, and polished so it shone like a mirror.

He looked out at the stars again. There was no sign of Orion at all; if it hadn't been for the sword, William would have been sure it had all been a dream. Yet there was no denying the marvelous blade which rested so comfortably in his hands. It was well balanced. And even through his thick gloves he could feel a slight warmth coming from it. It made his fingers tingle as if they had been lightly frostbitten.

He was suddenly excited by the thought of showing the sword to Maggie. Of course he would tell her all about what had happened, though he was not yet certain that he wanted anyone besides her to know the whole story. He needed time to think.

Carefully, he examined the leather sheath. It was designed to be worn around the waist, but it was much too large for him. After considering the problem for a moment, he slipped the wide waistband over his head and under his left arm so that it hung across his chest. Then, after a last, wondering look at the sword, he slipped it into the sheath. It fit perfectly.

As he edged his way back along the hull toward the airlock hatch, he tried to understand what had happened. It had all taken place so fast that his head spun. According to his watch, he had only been outside for fifteen minutes. In that short time, it seemed as if he had suddenly been swept into an eerie, interstellar game with the Genesis and her passengers as stakes. If he played well, if he were the winner, then the Genesis still had a chance for survival. But why had Orion chosen *him* above all the other colonists? There were many brave men aboard who could handle a sword better than he. He felt warm with pride when he thought of what Orion had said—that he, William Murdock, had the strongest heart. Yet he could scarcely believe it. Why should Orion want to help the colonists? Who was he? How could he live in space and move through the void without a jet gun?

The airlock was closer now. It was hard work groping his way along the railing with the huge sword hanging from his shoulder, but he was more used to his surroundings now and less frightened by them. That wonderful sword! Starnight—Orion had called it. Where could it have come from? Who cast it and polished it? And where had Orion himself come from? Why should the Watchers want to test William? He could only guess.

At last William's hand was on the wheel of the hatch. He stopped to catch his breath. Getting back inside the ship was going to be much riskier than getting out had been, for this time he had no way of knowing when the maintenance control officer's attention might be wandering. He would just have to take his chances and hope nobody noticed.

A glance at the pressure gauge on the outside of the

27

hull reassured him that the lock was still empty of air, so without further hesitation he pulled open the hatch and climbed up into the cubicle.

After he had resealed the hatch and opened the valves which would allow air to flow back into the lock, he climbed up to the inside bulkhead and anxiously rested his helmet against it, listening for telltale sounds of his discovery beyond. But he could hear nothing except the distant hum of the Genesis' power plant.

When the pressure inside the airlock was back to normal, he eagerly removed his helmet and breathed deeply. The air was dry and fresh compared to that inside his suit, which was humid and too warm after his adventure on the hull.

Pulling the marvelous sword out of its sheath once more, he sat down on a narrow, metal bench along one bulkhead. All thoughts of the maintenance control officer disappeared as he looked at his new treasure in amazement. The intricate engravings on its blade and handle looked clearer now. There were pictures of alien landscapes and strange creatures, along with symbols and what appeared to be complex mathematical diagrams.

He ran his gloved hand over the warm blade. Deep inside he had a growing feeling that Starnight was very old and somehow very powerful. What ancient beings were responsible for its creation? The question dazzled him like a cluster of suns.

He sat for a long while dreaming up possible histories for Starnight. It was not until a sharp clicking noise startled him that he realized with dismay that someone was opening the inner airlock hatch! Frantically, he looked about for a place to hide, but the tiny room offered no refuge. His breath caught as he watched the hatch swing slowly up.

Crowded around its circular border he could see several faces. One of them was Maggie's, small and pale with fright, and one was Captain Stone's. He could not quite see the other face, but it looked like one of the ship's councilmen. He knew immediately that he was in real trouble. His worst fears had come true. Someone must have seen the light on the maintenance panel. He had been discovered!

His heart banged emptily in his chest. What would he tell them? And, more important, what would become of Starnight?

Chapter Four

The Unexpected Friendship

"William Murdock," called the captain, his voice rumbling down hollowly from the storage room above.

William stood as if bolted to the floor of the airlock, his fingers tightening on the hilt of the sword where it hung below his left shoulder. He was afraid to speak. He wondered what would happen when he tried to explain.

"Mister Murdock, please come out of there. We wish to speak with you." The captain's voice was polite and businesslike, but it contained a thunderous undercurrent that sent tingles running up the back of William's neck.

Giving Starnight's hilt one last squeeze for good luck, William looked up at Captain Stone's furrowed, ruddy face and answered firmly, "Yes, sir." Pushing up from the airlock floor, he drifted through the hatch and into the storage room where the captain, another officer, and a member of the council waited with Maggie.

Something about the important faces in the group made him worry. Usually, when ship's rules were broken, the incident was taken care of by the sergeant-at-arms or the group of colonists that happened to be on police duty that week. It was very unusual for the captain himself to come down off the bridge for a thing like this. It was even more unusual for a councilman to be involved. It could mean that he was in worse trouble than he had thought.

The captain helped him up through the hatch, placing his large hand on William's shoulder to steady him as he climbed upward.

"Thank you, sir," said William as he turned to face the officers.

Before anyone could say another word, the councilman reached forward and grabbed William's arm roughly. "Why, you little idiot!" he shouted, his flabby face red with anger. "You're probably covered with those filthy little creatures! You've contaminated the whole ship!"

William clutched Starnight's handle wordlessly, too surprised to speak.

"Get your hands off the boy, Zerski," rumbled Captain Stone, seizing the councilman's wrist. "If you can't behave with any dignity, then please leave. I didn't ask you to come here in the first place. Politics is your job, not discipline."

Zerski flashed an ugly scowl at the captain, then let go of William's arm. "I'll make you sorry for this, Stone," he said, curling his puffy lips. "And you!" He turned toward William savagely. "You'll pay for this. Don't think you'll get away with contaminating this ship."

"Get out of here, Zerski. Now!" said the captain, his voice ominously low. "See him to the corridor, Mr. Jackson," he added, motioning to the officer.

"Yes, sir," replied Jackson. "Please come with me, Mr. Zerski." He took the councilman by the arm.

"Don't touch me," snarled Zerski. Sniffing, he stepped through the storage room hatch, followed by Jackson.

William, Maggie, and Captain Stone were left alone in the small storage chamber. "Well," said the captain, squinting at William from under bushy, gray eyebrows, "I suggest you remove that suit and throw it down the recycling chute—helmet, too. Maggie and I will wait outside for you." With that he motioned Maggie through the doorway, then followed her out into the ferryboat hangar.

Inside the storage chamber, William placed Starnight on a bench where he could see it while he wriggled out of the uncomfortable space suit. As he undid buckles and zippers, he watched the wonderful sword's handle change colors from hot white to fiery orange and back again. It seemed almost alive. The thought of having it taken away from him was almost too much to bear. He would have hidden it safely away somewhere in the storage chamber before he went out, but he was sure the captain had already noticed it, and he did not want to get into any more trouble by trying to lie about it.

After disposing of his suit he slipped the sheath over his shoulder and walked out into the hangar. Uneasily, he wondered about Councilman Zerski's accusations. What if he really *had* contaminated the ship?

He swallowed hard as he approached the captain and Maggie. Maggie's eyes were big with fear and her freckles stood out clearly on her pale face. He winked at her as cheerfully as he could, hoping to reassure her.

The captain let out a long breath through his teeth. "Hmmm," he said. "Well, I suppose you should tell me your story. From the beginning, with *nothing* left out. And for your sake, it had best be good." His great, bushy eyebrows met in a furrow. "And remember," he added,

"I've been around a long time. I know a lie when I hear one. Now, you can start by telling me what it is you've got dangling from your shoulder there."

"But, sir," began William hesitantly, "shouldn't I tell you the rest, first? You won't understand."

The captain was stern. "Maybe I'll understand and maybe I won't. Let me be the judge of that." His face softened a little, and the hint of a smile crossed his lips. "Come, Mr. Murdock. Quit shaking. I'm not some monster bent on having you for breakfast. I'm simply curious."

William gulped. "Yes, sir," he said. Slowly he drew the great sword out of its sheath and held it up for the captain and Maggie to see.

He heard Maggie draw in a sharp breath. "Oh, William!" she exclaimed, her eyes glowing. "It's beautiful."

The captain, too, seemed stunned. "Yes," he said quietly, "that it is."

For a moment the three of them watched Starnight as it changed color, its intricate engravings seeming almost to move by themselves in the glowing light.

"Where'd you get it?" whispered Captain Stone. "That's a treasure. Not something you just find floating in space. There's never been anything like it aboard this ship before!"

"Outside," answered William softly. "A great, golden man who called himself Orion gave it to me."

The captain turned sharply, piercing him with a gaze like steel.

"Oh, William," he heard Maggie gasp. "Then it's true! We *did* see him!"

"Do you mean to say, Mr. Murdock," rumbled the captain, "that you met up with something out there besides the metal bugs?"

"Yes, sir," answered William, relieved, for something in the captain's voice spelled belief.

"Hmmm," said Captain Stone. "I'd like to look over this sword of yours if I could."

"Of course," replied William, though every bit of him protested against the idea of letting Starnight go.

The captain reached for the sword, but his hand stopped suddenly, as if it had a mind of its own. A look of puzzlement swept across his face. "That's odd," he said. "I can't seem to touch it."

William tried to hand the sword to the captain, but discovered that he couldn't move his arms. Starnight stayed where it was. "I don't understand," he said, bewildered.

Suddenly, great waves of thunderous laughter filled the hangar. Maggie jumped. "What's that?" she cried.

Captain Stone reached for the stun pistol at his hip and looked around warily. "Who's there?" he shouted.

But William recognized the laughter immediately. "Orion!" he cried. "Where are you?" But the golden giant was nowhere to be seen.

"William Murdock." Orion's huge, deep voice seemed to come from everyplace at once. "No man may touch this sword unless you truly desire it."

"Orion!" cried William. "Come back! We need you." But there was no answer. The shadowy hangar deck was silent.

"Murdock," said Captain Stone, his eyes glowing with excitement, "tell me this story, and be quick about it. I want to know exactly what this is all about, right from the start."

They began the story slowly, William doing most of the talking and Maggie occasionally adding facts that he had passed over. They told about the hull puncture in the Earth chamber, and of their despair over the Genesis' predicament. Then they detailed their encounter with Orion in the observation cone. Maggie explained how they'd worked together to get William outside without attracting the attention of the maintenance control officer. Finally, William described his adventures with the gigantic golden man outside on the hull.

"Is Councilman Zerski right about my contaminating the ship?" William asked anxiously.

The captain's pleasant, ruddy features twisted into a frown. "Zerski seldom thinks things through before speaking," he said. "Contaminated? It's been contaminated for years. Every time a maintenance crew goes out they bring thousands of the creatures back inside with them. It was happening long before we even realized there was a problem." The captain snorted. "If Zerski paid attention to what was going on around him, he'd know that the one thing we *have* found out about metal bugs is that they don't like a lot of air pressure. It doesn't kill them, but it keeps them from multiplying." He laid a rough hand on William's shoulder. "So you needn't worry about that," he finished.

"Thank goodness," said William.

"Besides," Captain Stone added, "it sounds as if you have other things to worry about now. It's a strange tale you've both told me—very strange. And I can say with certainty that if I hadn't seen and heard proof just now, I wouldn't believe a word of it."

He rubbed his grizzled chin, looking first at William and then at Maggie. "You're in big trouble, especially with Zerski against you, now. You'll have to appear before the council, and he'll stop at nothing to see that you're punished." He shook his head. "For Zerski, things are black and white. You've broken a rule, no matter what the reasons. He's sworn that you'll pay for it, and in order to save face, he'll see that you *do.*"

Maggie looked frightened. "What will happen to us?" she asked shakily.

The captain broke into an unexpected smile. "What will happen to you? Nothing too bad, if I have anything to say about it." He looked strong and confident. "I intend to be a witness for you. We know what is at stake. If this golden man of yours has really offered us help, then it's the last hope we have of survival." He grew serious again. "You must be free to do what you have to in order to save this ship. If you are our only hope, then we can't allow you to be stopped. I'll see to it that the hearing is a fair one, at least."

William and Maggie burst into smiles. "Thank you, Captain Stone!" cried Maggie. "I knew you'd help us."

"Nonsense," said the captain gruffly. "I'll do what I must to help save the Genesis."

"You won't be sorry," said William gravely.

Captain Stone's face grew softer, and his gray eyes seemed to be looking at something far, far away. "No, I won't be sorry," he said quietly. "Too many people think that children are weak and helpless. But I remember. I know how strong a child can be—much stronger and wiser than the rest of us, sometimes. You won't fail us."

He turned and looked at them, smiling again. "Well," he said. "I believe you two have earned a cup of coffee in the captain's cabin. How does that sound?"

"Oh, boy!" shouted Maggie clapping her hands with glee.

William's cheeks were hot with pride. "Sounds great, sir," he said, unable to contain a wide smile.

Chapter Five

Trouble Strikes

After coffee, Captain Stone allowed William and Maggie to go back to their family cabin in Wheel I, but not before he'd given them a stern warning.

"You're not to go out on the hull again without asking my permission first," he cautioned. "You can't afford to get into any more trouble."

"Yes, sir," answered William.

As they stood to go out into the corridor, the captain put his hand on William's shoulder. "You're our last hope," he said. "We won't let that bothersome old Zerski stop you, so don't worry. I saw enough to convince *me*, and I'm going to tell the council that."

William and Maggie thanked the captain, shook his hand, then started down the quiet, carpeted hallway toward the Murdocks' cabin.

William hoped that no one would notice the sword. He had a feeling that it would be safer if he kept it as much a secret as possible. "We have to think of a good hiding place for Starnight," he said to Maggie as they walked along.

"I agree," she replied, vigorously nodding.

"And another thing," said William, stopping before the door to their cabin. Glancing up and down the corridor, he made sure no one was listening. "We're going to make a pact."

Maggie's face lit up with excitement. "A pact!" she exclaimed. "What kind?"

"We'll solemnly swear on this sword that we won't tell another living soul about it—not even mom and dad—until the hearing."

"But, William!" Maggie seemed shocked. "We'll *have* to tell mom and dad. How will we explain?"

But William would not be swayed. "Look, Maggie," he said, "this is important; it's big. It doesn't matter who the person is. We can't tell *anybody*. Even mom and dad might try to take the sword if they knew about it."

"But they can't," said Maggie. "You saw what happened when Captain Stone tried to touch it. Nobody can take Starnight unless you want them to."

"That doesn't matter," hissed William impatiently. Then, in exasperation, he added, "Maggie, I can't explain it. Just trust me. I have a feeling that we shouldn't tell anybody else about this unless we absolutely have to."

"Well," said Maggie uncertainly, "well...all right, I guess." Hesitantly she reached toward the sheath, then drew her hand back again. "Can I touch it?" she asked.

"Of course," smiled William. "You're my partner in this. Now put your hand on Starnight and we'll swear an oath." He looked around again to see if anybody was watching, but there was no one to be seen. Drawing the sword from its sheath he held it toward Maggie.

"Repeat after me," he said, as Maggie laid her hand on the glowing blade. "I swear on my honor that I will keep

the secret of Starnight from every living soul until the hearing."

Maggie repeated it slowly, her blue eyes flashing. William knew by the look on her face that she meant to keep the secret, whatever the cost. He could trust her.

Carefully he sheathed the sword again. "Come on," he said, smiling. "We have to find Starnight a good, safe hiding place before mom and dad come."

Together they walked through the sliding door and into the Murdock family cabin. Once inside, they briefly discussed hiding places.

"It has to be someplace no one will ever think of—someplace in this cabin where no one looks but you and me," said William.

"Hmmm..." answered Maggie. "That'll be hard. I don't know if there is such a place in the cabin."

William scratched his head. "I don't know either," he said, "but there must be someplace where no one would notice it for two or three days."

"I've got it!" cried Maggie, snapping her fingers. "Oh, this will be fun!" Her face glowed with enthusiasm.

"What is it?" asked William impatiently.

"I read this book once. A robber hid his sack of loot inside an air duct. William, if you could get the grill off the duct in our room, that would be a perfect place for Starnight. If you keep the sheath on, nobody will ever look there!"

William laughed and slapped his knee. "That's perfect!" he cried, and gave Maggie a big hug. "Just perfect."

Grabbing Starnight, he rushed into the room where he and Maggie slept. Swiftly he climbed onto one of the beds and worked his fingers under one edge of the air duct grill. It didn't take him long to pry it loose. "This will be just fine," he said, peering down the dark airway. A slight breeze with the faint, pleasant odor of plants and trees blew softly in his face. Deep in the maze of hallways in the main hull of the Genesis, the filtration system was hard at work purifying and recycling air in every chamber of the ship. He breathed deeply. He loved the fragrance of living things. It made his heart beat fast with the hope that someday he would live to see a planet, feel solid land beneath his feet, and watch a sun move slowly across a real sky.

Double checking to see that it was sheathed, he lifted the sword up into the duct and carefully moved it back a few inches from where the grill would go. When he felt sure that no one could see Starnight from the room below, he snapped the metal covering back into place and climbed down to the floor.

"Just right," he said to Maggie. "I'm sure it's the safest possible place."

"I hope so," said Maggie, "because a lot is going to depend on that sword. It's the only real way we have of proving that you went outside for a very good reason."

William nodded.

Just then, however, they heard the cabin door open and close. The sound of their parents' voices came from the living room.

"Don't forget," whispered William. "We made a pact."

"Don't worry," replied Maggie. "I won't tell, no matter what."

When he opened his eyes the next morning, William had an uneasy feeling. What could be causing it? He wondered as he lay quietly in his dark bedroom. He turned to look at Maggie. She was still sleeping deeply. He tried to pinpoint the cause of his anxiety but, still confused from sleep, he had a hard time. Everything seemed to look fine. The room was still as orderly as it was when he'd gone to bed. He couldn't smell anything unusual. The air seemed clear and fresh as always.

Then he realized that there was an odd sound coming from outside the cabin. At this hour of the morning the only noises should have been the steady hum of the power plant and the soft gurgling of the dehumidifier coils. Instead, William heard voices coming from the corridor—a lot of voices, some of them very high and loud. Something was wrong!

He jumped out of bed without putting on his robe and, clad only in pajamas, ran through the cabin door and out into the corridor. He hesitated a moment, looking down the hallway, first in one direction and then in the other. The lamps were still quite dim, and wouldn't be up to daytime strength for at least another hour, but even in the half-light, William could make out a small knot of people a few meters away.

"What happened?" cried one of them.

"I don't know. We were just walking along and suddenly—" said another, but was interrupted before he had time to finish.

"What did you do to him?" demanded someone.

"Nothing! I swear it."

Cautiously, William moved toward the commotion. "Is somebody hurt?" he asked, but got no answer. He stood for several minutes trying to peer between the onlookers to see what was happening. In a moment he could see that there was a man lying on the floor. He was unable to tell who it was.

"Well, let's not just stand here," someone said. "I'll call the sick bay."

Before long, two orderlies on an ambulance cart arrived with a stretcher.

"Get back, everybody," said one of them. "Give us room to work."

The orderlies worked swiftly and efficiently, lifting the man onto their stretcher and carefully covering him with a bright blanket. William's curiousity was growing. Who could it be?

"Who is it?" he asked the man who stood next to him.

The man looked down. The expression on his face made William uncomfortable. For a moment he thought the man was going to order him back to his cabin. "What are you doing out in the corridor at this hour dressed like that?" he asked.

Suddenly William realized that he had on only his pajamas. "I—I heard voices," he replied in embarrassment.

The man looked toward the busy orderlies. "It's Captain Stone," he said. "I think he's ill."

"Captain Stone!" cried William in dismay. "But—he'll be all right, won't he?"

"I don't know," was the answer. "He looks pretty bad."

As William watched, the orderlies moved the stretcher onto the ambulance cart. For the first time, he got a good look at the motionless figure wrapped in the blanket. Yes. It *was* Captain Stone. His face was a frightening grayish color. His eyes were closed, and from time to time he groaned and mumbled words that William could not understand. William felt as if he were in the midst of a nightmare. He could not move, and a cold, swirling horror began to grow inside him.

"But the captain *has* to be all right," he whispered. "The hearing... without him, they'll find me guilty. They'll smash our last hope."

"What?" asked the man as if he had not been paying attention. "Speak up."

William shivered. "Oh, nothing," he answered. "Nothing."

He felt suddenly miserable and foolish in the dim corridor. "I shouldn't be here," he murmured, and turned to go back to the cabin.

Chapter Six

Fighting the Council

William shuffled back into the cabin, closed the door and slumped dazedly on the sofa. It was still dark. The morning lamps had not come on yet, and the only light was the soft glow of stars from the cabin's small porthole.

He rested his chin moodily in his hands and stared out into space. He remembered the silence of the observation cone, the eerie light of stars, and the glowing figure of Orion as he beckoned from outside. He was hurt and bewildered. Where was Orion now? How could he expect William to convince the officers and councilmen of the Genesis that he was telling the truth? They all saw him as an unimportant child with too big an imagination— all but the captain, and now the captain was stricken with a mysterious illness. If he didn't recover soon, not even *he* could help.

The only way William could prove his story now was with the sword. The thought of Starnight safe in its leather sheath behind the air duct grill made him feel

47

somewhat brighter. Once the councilmen had seen that magnificent sword, they would *have* to believe him.

In the darkness, he groped toward the storage drawer where his father kept a small energy lamp for emergencies. Pointing the lamp down at the floor, he crept back into his bedroom and climbed stealthily onto his bed. Maggie was still asleep, and he could hear her even breathing from the other side of the room. As he reached toward the grill, he could feel cool, fresh air in his face, and his mind leaped at the thought that soon he might be standing on a planet enjoying delicious air that was *always* fresh, *always* scented with a hundred smells of free living things, forever clean with washings of rain and wind.

Eagerly he tugged at the grill, holding the light with one hand and prying with the other. At last the metal came away and William flashed his lamp into the open air duct.

But he could see nothing except bare steel! What had happened? Squinting with disbelief, he thrust his hand into the air duct. *Starnight was gone!*

"Oh, no!" he cried. His throat was suddenly tight and hot and he struggled to keep back tears.

"What?" Maggie's voice was slow and scratchy with sleep. She sat up. "What's the matter?"

William dropped to his knees on the bed. "Starnight," he moaned. "It's gone."

"Gone?" Maggie bolted out of her covers and stood on her tiptoes to see inside the duct. "What could have happened?" she cried.

William couldn't speak. He could only sit in bewilderment and fight to keep from crying.

Maggie sat down beside him and put her small arm across his shoulders. "William," she said, "don't worry. We'll find whoever did this, and we'll get Starnight back, even if we have to tear the Genesis apart. I'll bet it was that creepy Zerski."

William shook his head. "It couldn't be Zerski," he said numbly. "Nobody knew about the hiding place except you and I. Nobody could have found it."

A terrible thought occurred to him. "It could have been Orion. He's the only one who could have seen us hide it. It *had* to be him. I knew there was something funny about him from the very beginning. He acted strange from the start."

The morning lamps were beginning to brighten. He could see Maggie's face dimly as it twisted into an odd expression that was almost a frown. "No, I don't think it was Orion," she said slowly. "I have a feeling that we can trust him—I don't know why."

The look on her face was so strange that William was suddenly worried. "Are you all right?" he asked.

As if he pushed some invisible button, the odd look disappeared from Maggie's face. "Oh," she said, as if she herself were startled. "Yes, I'm fine."

After a moment's hesitation William said, "It's bad enough that Starnight's disappeared. But there's something that makes it even worse. Captain Stone has suddenly become very ill. I saw them take him to sick bay on an ambulance cart early this morning."

"Sick?" exclaimed Maggie in horror. "But he was just fine yesterday. What happened?"

William shrugged. "I don't know. He was unconscious. And unless he's better by this afternoon, we won't have a chance at that hearing."

Maggie looked as if she, too, wanted to cry. "I can't believe it," she whispered. "Nobody can have this much bad luck. I'm telling you, it's that Zerski. He's a very bad man."

"No," said William. "That's impossible. No matter how bad Zerski is, he couldn't have found Starnight, and he wouldn't do anything to the captain. He has too much to lose. He would be finished if they caught him doing anything like that to the ship's highest officer."

"Well, the captain will be all right, won't he?" asked Maggie.

"I don't know," answered William. "He sure looked bad."

Maggie said nothing.

Later that afternoon, the Murdocks walked quickly down the long corridor of Wheel I on their way to the council chambers.

"Straighten your collar, dear," chided William's mother.

"Yes, mother," replied William, gloomily. He seldom wore his best coveralls. They were stiff and scratchy. He pulled uncomfortably on the high collar, wishing desperately that somehow he could have opened that airlock hatch without anyone finding out about it.

"Leave the child alone," William heard his father say to his mother with a stormy look in his deep eyes. His voice was too low and rough. "He has enough to worry about without fooling with his collar." He looked down sternly at William. "Like disgracing the whole family with his antics."

As they stopped before the shiny door of the council chamber, Maggie whispered, "William, everything will be fine. I just heard one of the officers say that Captain Stone is going to be all right. He'll talk to the council over the intercom, and they'll *have* to believe him."

William smiled, nodding. He wished he felt as confident as Maggie.

At that moment, the chamber door slid ominously

open and he gulped as he got a glimpse of the council members sitting proudly in their black robes. The bailiff, whose son was a friend of William's, winked and smiled encouragingly as he showed them into the chamber and directed them to a row of seats in the front. William waited impatiently as the head councilman brought the hearing to order.

The head councilman had been old for as long as William could remember. He had always been furrowed and crinkled. The man's pale skin reminded William of the fine, milky flour that poured from the stones in the ship's grist mill when a harvest of wheat was in from one of the Genesis' farms. His face looked soft like the flour, and his wrinkles almost seemed to be filled with dust.

His head wobbled on his thin shoulders when he spoke. "William Murdock, come to the bench," he said with a hint of a smile on his thin, dry lips.

William stood, feeling shaky but determined to tell the truth at all costs. He walked through the gate and up to the wooden podium with the councilmen's cold gazes heavy upon him. There was a wicked gleam in Zerski's eyes.

"Well, now, William. I have here a complaint that states that you went outside the ship yesterday without permission. Is that true?" said the old man.

"Yes, sir," answered William.

"What have you to say for yourself?" said the chief councilman as he ruffled the edge of the paper that lay on the podium before him.

"I know I broke the rules, sir, but I had a good reason." And William told the council the whole story of Orion just as he had explained it to Captain Stone the day before.

The old councilman frowned at him, disbelief etched into every line of his withered face. "Very well, William," he grumbled. "And have you any evidence to show that your story is true, and not just a falsehood designed to keep you from being punished? Show us this sword, for example."

William gulped and fingered the top button on his collar which suddenly seemed tighter and scratchier than ever. "Your Honor, I'm sorry, but the sword has disappeared," he said.

This brought undisguised laughter from the entire council. William's face was hot and his heart pounding with anger and humiliation. Zerski snickered gleefully. "There never was a sword."

All at once William heard Maggie cry loudly from behind him. "Don't say that! William's telling the truth and you know it, Mr. Zerski. You saw Starnight, too!"

"Yes," added William. "Besides that, Maggie saw Orion. And Captain Stone can tell you the sword was real, too. He saw it with his own eyes after I came out of the airlock."

The laughter stopped abruptly as the chief councilman raised his gavel and tapped it on the podium before him, shouting for order.

"You may go to your seat, William," said the old man severely. "And you, young lady." He beckoned toward Maggie. "You may come forward and tell us what you have to say, in an orderly manner."

"I object," cried councilman Zerski, rising from his seat. "You know she'll do nothing but lie for her brother. This whole story is nothing but a fairy tale. *I* was there, and I saw no sword."

"Perhaps," said the chief councilman. "But I wish to hear her. And so would you if you took the time to think about it. We are here to judge fairly and to hear all sides of this story."

William took his seat and Maggie stepped forward with a toss of her reddish-blond curls.

"All right, Margaret," said the chief councilman when she stood before him. "Even a person as young as you must know how great a crime it is to lie to the council. You must tell me the absolute truth and not make up any stories for your brother. Is that clear?"

"Yes," said Maggie soberly. "Yesterday afternoon, William and I were in the observation cone together when I saw something move outside. At first, I wasn't sure what it was, but then it came back again and William saw it, too. It was a big, golden man—Orion. William wanted to go outside right away, because Orion was motioning to him. I didn't want him to go but I had to give in, finally, even though I was afraid he would get caught." She hesitated a moment, then went on. "The next time I saw William, he was coming out of the airlock in the ferry boat hangar. Captain Stone and Mr. Zerski saw him come out, too. He was carrying a big sword like nothing I've ever seen before. Captain Stone tried to touch it, but Orion's voice came out and said nobody but William—"

"Just a moment, Margaret," interrupted the chief councilman, shaking his head. "I'm afraid we've heard enough of this story."

Maggie's eyes flashed as her quick temper got out of hand. William held his breath as she retorted, "You think I'm lying, don't you?"

The old man pounded his gavel on the podium again as he rumbled, "Miss Murdock, hold your tongue. Sit down, before I find you in contempt. If your story is true, then Captain Stone will verify it. If it is not, then both you and your brother will be punished!"

Biting her lip, Maggie turned and walked back to her seat. William smiled at her in an effort to reassure her, but Mr. Murdock grabbed her firmly by the arm and settled her roughly into her chair. His face was hard with anger. The children were silent. William knew from experience that when that look was on his father's brow, talking only made things worse.

"Bailiff," called the head councilman, "get us an intercom connection with the sick bay."

In a few seconds, the council intercom screen glowed with the pleasant face of the ship's surgeon, Dr. Curtis.

"Doctor," said the head councilman, "can you connect us with Captain Stone? We have a matter of some importance here and we must speak to him."

"Well," frowned Dr. Curtis, "I have prescribed complete rest for the captain. Can't this wait?"

"No," answered the old man, "I'm afraid it can't. But we will only take a few moments."

"Very well," said the doctor.

His face disappeared, and in its place was Captain Stone's, looking weary and drawn.

"What can I do for you?" he asked.

"We are hearing the matter of William Murdock, the boy who was caught outside the ship yesterday. He tells us you have some information that might help him."

"Murdock," said the captain. "A wonderful boy." There was a far away look in his eyes, as if he were struggling to remember something. "I—" he began, "I know I was there when he came out of the airlock, but...but I just can't remember what happened." He wrinkled his forehead. "I'm extremely sorry," he said, apologetically. "I've been ill."

"We understand," said the old councilman, shaking his head in sympathy. "Thank you."

The captain's face disappeared from the screen.

William's heart sank as the head councilman banged his gavel again. "Very well. Council will repair to chambers to decide on this matter."

Chapter Seven

The Ghost Lock

William trudged glumly down the corridor toward sick bay. The message he had gotten from the captain that afternoon requested that William go and visit him when school was over. There was nothing he could do. He couldn't turn down a request from Captain Stone. It just wasn't done.

He smiled a bit, thinking of the looks on the other kids' faces when his teacher, Mr. Masataka, had said, "William, I have a note for you from the captain." He was getting quite a reputation at school—almost like some kind of wild hero. Sometimes he liked it and sometimes he didn't.

He was sorry about the way the hearing had turned out. His sentence could have been worse, it was true. The chief councilman had said the punishment should probably have lasted three months considering that William had not only gone outside without permission but had also lied about it afterward. William could remember clearly how the old man had smiled when he'd said that the weeding sessions were only to last for six weeks. The council had decided that William was basically a good child, in spite of his mistakes. Even Maggie had gotten a share in the punishment. She had to help in the Wheel I kitchen for an hour each day. It made him angry just to think about how unfair it had all been.

Yet he didn't really mind spending two hours each afternoon weeding on the Wheel I vegetable farm. He liked the feel of the moist soil in his hands. He even liked the way it smelled, rich with plant life. It wasn't so bad. Worse punishment by far was the idea that his wonderful dream of saving the Genesis had been utterly shattered.

He had already served two weeks of his sentence. Still, he had not seen Starnight since the evening he had hidden it behind the grill of the air duct. He had not seen Orion again either, even though he watched for him every evening in the observation cone. Sadly, he began to wonder if the whole incident had ever really happened. It seemed as if everything was going against him.

Now he stood reluctantly before the sick bay door. What would he say to the captain? The captain had smashed William's last hope of saving the ship. It was hard to believe that his memory had failed him on such an important point. William sometimes wondered if Zerski hadn't talked Captain Stone into "forgetting," somehow. Yet he didn't want to believe that.

He rang the bell on the door and fumbled in his pocket for the note the captain had sent.

A young nurse answered. "Yes?" she asked.

"Captain Stone wants to see me," said William, handing her the rumpled paper.

The nurse glanced at the note, raised her eyebrows, and said, "Oh, yes, William. Come in."

She showed him into the small, brightly painted cubicle where Captain Stone lay in bed, studying star charts. "Right in here," she said, and hurried off.

"Ah, Mr. Murdock," said the captain smiling and looking over the tops of his reading glasses. "I've been waiting for you. Glad you came." He motioned to a nearby chair. "Won't you sit down?"

"Thank you, sir," said William.

"I was wondering how you and Maggie were," said Captain Stone. His face looked tired and thin.

"We're fine, sir," answered William, looking at the floor. He was afraid his eyes might give away the tenseness and anger he felt.

"Murdock, I..." the captain began. William was surprised to hear a sudden catch in his voice. He looked up to find that Captain Stone's cheeks were red. He was blushing! "This is very hard for me, you see."

"What is it, sir?" asked William in astonishment.

The captain folded his hands on his stomach. "I might as well get to the point. You know I'm not a man who takes much stock in hunches and feelings. But ever since your hearing, I've been bothered by the idea that I've somehow betrayed you."

William was silent, feeling awkward, and unsure of the proper response.

Captain Stone shook his head and frowned until his forehead looked like a newly-ploughed field. "I don't know how this could be," he continued. "It's as if a little piece of my memory had somehow been removed. You see, I cannot remember anything about what happened after you first came out of that airlock. Nothing. And yet I have the feeling that something very important happened—something you were counting on me to tell the council." He shrugged, looking uncomfortable. "I sometimes feel as if something—some terrible thing—has me clutched in its fist. Something is making me forget, and I don't know what it is."

"But," said William anxiously, "don't the doctors know what's wrong with you?"

The captain shook his head. "They have no idea. But whatever it is, it makes me weak and tired. I feel as if I've been fighting something for days on end. Something strong, and something very strange." He paused and looked piercingly at William. "Somehow," he said, "I think it has something to do with what happened that day outside the airlock."

William nodded. "Did you hear the things I said to the council?" he asked.

"No," said the captain. "The doctors said I was too weak to listen. And I haven't been able to get a copy of it to read yet."

"Well," said William, rising from his chair, "you are right, sir. I'm quite certain of it. The story's too long to tell you now, so I'll just say that everything I told the council is true. We're fighting strange, terrible powers, fighting for our lives. We have to win, or we'll die."

The captain seemed lost in his own thoughts. "If only I could remember," he murmured.

"Don't worry, sir," said William. "You'll remember." His mind was rushing like a river. A terrible, magnificent idea had just occurred to him. Quite unexpectedly, Orion's words of warning had come back to him.

"You can be sure I am telling you the truth when I say that there is great evil in this world, evil which sees you and knows of your presence here," Orion had said as he handed William the wonderful sword. Now it occurred to William that perhaps Captain Stone's mysterious illness could not be explained by ordinary means. In fact, nothing that had happened since that fateful day when William had first encountered Orion could be explained very easily. After all, things really couldn't be going much worse for William. Everything had gone wrong. He had been discovered coming out of the airlock, the sword had disappeared in spite of all his careful planning, and the one person the council would believe, Captain Stone, had been unable to testify for him. Not only that. Zerski had done everything in his power to make things rough on William. The chain of events was so ill-fated that it defied the ordinary rules of chance. Perhaps there were greater powers at work against him than he had thought!

"Well, Mr. Murdock," said the captain, interrupting William's reverie, "I hope we are still friends."

"Of course we are, sir," answered William, smiling. "And don't worry. You're going to get well."

"I hope you're right," replied the captain. He paused, rubbing his chin as if deep in thought. Then he added with a smile, "I'll be glad to write you an excuse from your weeding session today if you like."

"Thank you, sir," William answered, "but I don't really mind the work. It gives me time to think. I could use an excuse for being late, though."

"Fine," said Captain Stone, nodding in approval. "That's the spirit." Hastily, he jotted a note to the vegetable farm foreman. "Here you are." He handed it to William.

"Thank you again, sir," said William. "I'm glad I came."

"See you later, then." The captain shook his hand and William turned to leave.

During his weeding session that afternoon, he worked hard, hoping that if he kept busy, his supervisor would not interrupt him. He was alone and free to think over the

59

strange idea that had occurred to him while talking to Captain Stone. Orion's warning kept coming back to him. If this "great evil" of which the huge, golden man had spoken was able to control the captain, perhaps it had been instrumental in the disappearance of Starnight as well.

There were only two people on the ship who could have taken the sword from its secret hiding place. One was William himself, and the other was Maggie. He was nearly certain that he had not taken it, although if this evil force were really as powerful as it seemed to be, it could be possible. But what about Maggie?

Impatiently, William finished his garden work and hurried back to the family cabin. When he came in, Maggie was sitting on the livingroom floor playing a game of power jacks. He watched for a moment as she skillfully bounced the green ball and picked up the glowing, plastic cubes.

After a minute or two he whispered excitedly, "Are mom and dad home?"

"No," answered Maggie with a puzzled look. "Why are you whispering?"

"I've got to talk to you. It's about the sword, and no one else must hear," said William.

"There's nobody here but you and me," replied Maggie, frowning and fidgeting uneasily.

"Okay," said William quietly. "Look, Maggie. I've thought of something. I just talked to Captain Stone and he told me a very strange thing. He said the doctors don't know what is wrong with him. He really can't remember anything about what happened after I came out of the airlock. He said he felt like he was fighting something. Something very evil and very strong.

"Now listen carefully, and don't get the wrong idea about what I'm going to say. You and I were the only two

60

people who knew where Starnight was hidden, right?"

"Right," answered Maggie, nodding slowly and looking strangely frightened.

"That means that if someone took the sword, it was either you or I. It couldn't have been anyone else. Now suppose this 'thing' that made Captain Stone forget what he saw, also made one of us get into the air duct, take Starnight out, and hide it someplace. Maybe we wouldn't remember doing it. Do you see what I mean?"

When she looked up at him, William could see that her cheeks were bright and flushed, almost as if with fever. Suddenly she burst out, "Oh, William! I've been wanting to tell you this but I was afraid you wouldn't understand. The night before the council hearing, I dreamed that I got up and took the sword out and hid it someplace. At first, I was sure that it was just a dream. But now I really don't know anymore."

William squeezed Maggie's arm excitedly. "That was just what I was hoping for," he cried. "Maggie, do you remember what you did with Starnight in this dream? Because if you can remember that, maybe we can find it again."

Maggie rubbed her forehead. "I don't know, William," she said worriedly. "I've tried and tried to remember, but I just can't. The only thing I can remember is that I put the sword in a place that was dark and kind of—stuffy, or musty."

William frowned. What sort of place could that be? All the rooms he could think of aboard the Genesis were used often and were well lit. Of course, there were places that were dark. The observation cone was dark, for example. But he could not think of a place that was musty. The ship's air purification system supplied a steady stream of fresh air to every chamber. He thought hard. The two great wheels of the starship were out of the question. They were used as living and working quarters for the colonists and every cubic foot of space inside them was used daily for the activities that kept the ship going and kept the people aboard it supplied with the necessities of life.

Probably the sword was hidden someplace in the mammoth central hull. "Do you suppose you might have put it somewhere up in the main hold?" asked William.

"Well, yes. It's possible. Sometimes I have the feeling that I climbed a long flight of stairs," answered Maggie hesitantly.

William thought of the long, deserted stairways in the wheel spokes. Yes, that made sense. Maggie must have used them to get to the main hold without being seen. Still, the only place William could think of that fit her description was the observation cone. That would be a very poor hiding spot indeed, for the door to the cone was often left hanging open by the ship's maintenance crews. The sword would not be secret there for long.

Suddenly, William had an idea. He struck his forehead with the palm of his hand. "Maggie, why didn't I think of this before?"

"What?" said Maggie anxiously.

"Come on. I know the perfect place." And grabbing her by the hand, he rushed out into the corridor and down toward the nearest elevator.

The ride took only a few minutes. They went faster and faster as the huge counterweight of the elevator system fell down toward the wheel rim, carrying them at greater and greater speeds up into the ship's center.

When they stopped, William rushed out the door and flew like a bullet down the dimly lit corridor. Maggie, struggling to keep up, called after him, "Slow down, William! If we get caught going so fast in here, we'll be in trouble all over again!"

But William was filled with a driving energy that pulled him on and on toward the aft portion of the ship, where a certain deserted airlock lay. It was the only possible spot for the sword. The colonists referred to it as the "ghost lock"—a single chamber located on the firewall just in front of the twin exhaust cones of the Genesis' monstrous thrust rockets. There was no one alive who could remember the last time those rockets had spewed out fire. They had been silent now for hundreds of years. The Genesis traveled swiftly along its ancient course driven only by momentum now. The ghost lock had once been used by ship's engineers for maintenance of the huge rockets. But now the outside door was specially sealed and could be opened only with certain keys which the captain and the chief engineer possessed.

But there was one thing about the ghost lock which was very important to William. It was neither ventilated nor lighted!

At the small hatch of the airlock, William hesitated, confused and gasping for breath. A very unpleasant idea had just occurred to him. Naturally, if it were not in use, the room would also be unheated. William had read in a book that pieces of matter in deep space sometimes became so cold that their molecules contracted until they collapsed upon themselves. Only the heat produced by the ship's great nuclear power plants kept the Genesis itself from becoming so cold that its molecules would fall in, causing the ship to collapse into a tiny ball of matter. Still, the air inside that lock would be cold enough to kill William and anyone else nearby in just seconds unless they had on protective clothing.

At that moment, Maggie came sailing breathlessly up to him, her eyes wide as she panted with exertion. "I remember! I remember!" she cried, immediately. "Yes! I put Starnight in the ghost lock!"

"How could you remember, Maggie?" cried William in his sudden disappointment. "Why, all you had on was a nightgown. The air in there would have frozen you to death instantly!"

Maggie drew back, looking shocked and hurt. "There's no reason to get so mad," she retorted. "Maybe you don't know everything, William Murdock."

"Of course I don't know everything," cried William. "But you can't change the facts. If I open that door we'll both die." Through his pain and disappointment, he was ashamed of his shouting and of the things he said. But he could barely control himself. He wanted to hurt Maggie. Hurt her for stealing the sword, and for wanting him to kill them both by opening the airlock.

Suddenly the truth struck him. "Oh, my gosh," he whispered in despair, covering his eyes with one hand. "It's got me, too, hasn't it? Making me act this way when there's no reason to!"

He felt Maggie's small, warm hand on his shoulder. "It's all right, William," she said softly. "Starnight won't let us die."

He removed his hand in time to see her float to the airlock hatch and turn the wheel. "Don't, Maggie!" he screamed. What if it really was just a dream! What if Maggie never had taken the sword to begin with? What if the evil thing was making her open that hatch?

He lunged toward her in a desperate attempt to knock her away before the metal door swung out. But it was too late. A whoosh of cold air hit him and the dark airlock gaped open.

Chapter Eight

The Monstrous Test

In the next moment, time came almost to a stop for William. Everything seemed to happen in slow motion as he made up his mind that death was coming, and that there was no escape. His heart pounded like a huge piston within him as the hatch fell open at Maggie's touch and a sudden gush of cold, stale air rushed out into the main hold. William covered his face with his hands, waiting for his heart to stop completely.

But the puff of cool air passed in a second or two, time resumed its normal pace, and William took down his shaking hands to find before him a wonderful sight. The inside of the airlock glowed with a strange, warm display of colors that moved as if the chamber were filled with gently moving water! He nearly shouted with glee as he spied the wayward sword floating just beyond the hatchway, several inches from the deck, pulsing with the familiar orange light that followed it everywhere. Its sheath drifted beside it.

"Starnight!" he cried, lunging forward to seize its shining hilt.

"You see?" laughed Maggie, watching him from the hatchway. "I knew nothing bad would happen."

William paused, frowning in bewilderment. "Why wasn't that airlock cold, anyway?" he murmured, squinting at the bare metal walls. "I was certain..."

He gripped the sword tightly as his mistake became clear to him. "Of course," he said, looking up at Maggie. "How could I be so foolish? Space is a perfect insulator. It doesn't conduct heat or cold. It's like a giant thermos bottle. Even if that room were never heated again, it wouldn't get more than a few degrees cooler than the rest of the ship!" Immediately an ugly thought hit him. "I shouldn't have forgotten that. And I don't see how I could have forgotten if..."

Maggie nodded, almost as if she'd read his mind. "If *something* hadn't made you forget," she finished slowly.

William's knuckles grew white on the handle of the sword. An empty feeling filled his stomach. "We're really up against something big, aren't we, Maggie?" he said softly.

She nodded again, remaining silent in the open hatchway of the musty ghost lock.

"We've got to do something right away," said William. "We just can't wait any longer, not anymore. Something's trying to stop us and it *will* if we let it."

Maggie looked worried as she drifted beside him and ran her fingers lightly over the patterns on Starnight's blade. "But what can we do? We don't even know why Orion gave you the sword. We haven't any idea how to get these 'gleaming stones' he told you about. We don't know where to start."

William almost whispered his reply. "I don't know. I just can't figure it out. Orion said that at the right time it would all be clear. But maybe he was wrong. Maybe he shouldn't have chosen me after all. Things just don't seem to be going right at all."

Maggie looked at him fiercely. "Don't say those things, William. If it hadn't been for you, we would never have found Starnight again. Why, if it hadn't been for you, there wouldn't even be a chance for the Genesis. We'd be doomed to drift in space until all of us died!"

But William had lost the thread of her words before she finished. In horror he stared past her toward the airlock door.

"What's wrong?" said Maggie with a frightened quaver in her voice. She turned and gave a little shriek of terror. William felt her fingernails dig into his arm. There between him and Maggie and the safety of the ghost lock door stood a gigantic monster more horrible than anything that had ever walked in a nightmare.

The thing was blood red and shiny as if its skin were covered with slime. It had four arms ending in claws which seemed to burn white hot. It seemed to be squatting down so that its head, tiny and insect-like compared to its huge body, would not bump the airlock ceiling.

William pushed Maggie into the far corner of the chamber. "Get back!" he cried, squeezing the handle of the sword with all his might. He could hear the monster breathing, a nasty, rasping sound like the bellows of a colossal furnace.

He panted, feeling dizzy with fear. "Get out of here or I'll kill you," he shouted. His voice sounded pitiful and high. He was sorry he had spoken.

But the monster did not move. He sat squarely in the doorway, silent except for his fiery breathing.

William raised the sword wildly, frightened half out of his wits, trying to think of some way for Maggie to get out of the door and beyond the thing's reach. He would have to make a move—distract it. "Move, or I'll kill you!" he repeated, and started to lunge toward the monster with all the force he could muster.

The monster's crimson skin was only inches from Starnight's deadly point when William suddenly reached out and stopped himself against the bulkhead. Warily, he let down the sword.

"William, what's wrong?" he heard Maggie whisper behind him.

"I just thought of something," he said quietly, allowing himself to drift back a meter or two. He looked up toward the creature's small head.

"Monster, what do you want from us?" he asked loudly. "Why are you here?"

There was no answer, only the heavy breathing.

"Monster, you have done us no wrong. I don't want to kill you. But if you don't let us leave, then I will be forced to," said William.

At that, the monster moved his head so that William could see his gleaming eyes, like those of a tremendous fly. "I am fearsome," said the thing in a roaring voice. "Yet, you will not kill me?"

"No," said William, trembling, "not unless you try to hurt us."

The monster paused for a moment. William held his breath.

"Hear me, then," said the monster after what seemed an eternity. "I have a message for you."

"A message—again?" gasped William, thinking back to the first one, delivered to him by Orion. It seemed so long ago. The creature paid no attention to William's exclamation.

"By sparing me, you have passed the first test which the Watchers devised for you. If you can pass the second, then you have earned the right to their help. Listen now to my message, and be glad."

The monster paused again. The terrible sound of his raspy breathing filled the chamber. William listened tensely. "The hilt holds the key to Starnight's mistress, the swan," roared the beast.

Then, before either William or Maggie could say a word, there was a hollow, popping sound and the gigantic monster was gone without a trace!

William drifted—motionless and breathing hard. He heard Maggie come up behind him. "William, what did he mean?" she asked, her voice high and ragged with excitement.

"I don't know. I don't know," he murmured, his hands shaking as he fumbled with the sword. "Let me think."

He turned Starnight over and over, carefully examining its golden handle and the splendid, curving crosspiece designed to protect a warrior's hand in battle. "The swan," he whispered. "Who is the swan? What part of a sword handle could hold a key? And what sort of key would it be?"

He ran his fingers over the hilt, pushing and juggling at the various designs, watching for the opening of a trap door or the movement of a hidden button.

"Whew," he breathed. "If I could just get my hands to stop shaking. I can't find anything. The whole sword must be made out of one piece of metal."

He felt Maggie's hand on his shoulder. "It's okay. I wouldn't care if you shook from now till doomsday. You're the best, bravest person in the world!"

He shrugged in embarrassment. "Maggie, you just shouldn't say things like that." He pushed her hand away. "If you only knew how scared I was. This whole thing scares the living daylights out of me."

Maggie watched silently as he squinted up and down

the shining blade. "There's something in the back of my mind. I just can't quite remember what it is—but it has something to do with swans," he muttered, shaking his head.

"I wonder what it could be," said Maggie, pursing her lips as if to help her think.

"I don't know. But it might have been something I heard at school—maybe something Mr. Masataka said." William sighed and looked up at the lovely, colored reflections of Starnight's eerie light that played on the walls. "Oh, if only I could think," he said. "We're getting so close!"

"Hmmm," said Maggie. "Something your teacher said? It must have been during biology if it was about swans."

"No, I don't think so," answered William slowly. His mind was whirling and it seemed impossible to get his thoughts straight. Silently, he tried to make his heart slow down, but it galloped in spite of him.

"William." Maggie's voice was gentle. "You look so tired. Maybe you'd be able to think better if we went back to the cabin."

He smiled halfheartedly. "Yes, I guess you're right. If we stay here, we're bound to be missed, and someone will come looking for us. That's the last thing we need."

He slipped Starnight into its leather sheath. The ghost lock was plunged into semi-darkness without the sword's pulsing light. "We'd better go down by the stairs," said William.

But Maggie grabbed his arm before he could move toward the hatch. "If somebody sees us carrying Starnight through the corridors, there'll be a lot of questions asked. Word will get around. Everybody will know about it within two hours."

"I hadn't thought of that," replied William. "But I'm sure you're right. Maybe we should find something to wrap Starnight up in—a blanket, or something. That way, if anybody *does* see us, they might not bother to ask us what we're doing."

"Well, let's see," said Maggie. "What can we use?"

William looked out into the dim corridor, straining to see. The walls were bare metal and offered nothing. He knew that there were storerooms along the corridor, and that they contained all sorts of bedding and extra clothing, but all of them were kept locked. Besides, they were guarded from the maintenance control officer's panel, just as the airlock had been when William went outside to find Orion.

But only a few doors down was another corridor. It led deep into the very heart of the ship, to the engineering decks. There the Genesis' great, nuclear engines lay, humming their deep, muffled work song. There, dozens of colonists labored each day and all through the night, to maintain the intricate machinery which supplied the ship with power. Jobs on the engineering decks often involved hard, grimy work, so the designers of the Genesis had equipped her aft section with a large locker room where the engineers could shower and clean up after their shifts. The locker room was stocked with lots of big towels, *and it was unguarded!*

"That's it!" cried William, turning to Maggie.

"That's what? Have you thought of a way to hide Starnight?" she asked.

"Yes," he answered. "We'll get a towel from the engineers' locker room."

"Super!" cried Maggie, clapping her hands. "That's perfect."

"Okay. Here's what we'll do," said William. "You stay

71

here to make sure that nothing happens to the sword, and I'll go get the towel."

But Maggie shook her head quickly. "No, William. I don't think I should stay here alone. What if . . . well, what if I stole the sword again without knowing? Then we'd be right back where we started from. We just haven't got the time for mishaps like that anymore."

William thought about it for a moment. Maggie was right. It would be risky to leave her here alone. The rate of hull punctures had already risen sharply; the atmosphere was becoming thinner with each passing hour. In two or three days, there would be nothing left to save inside the Genesis. Whatever they did, they would have to do it soon. There was no time to waste.

"All right, Maggie," he said at last. "You go get the towel. But hurry. And don't let anyone see you if you can help it."

"Don't worry," she called as she rushed off down the corridor. "I can do it."

Alone, William sat quietly. Once again he drew the sword out of its sheath. Its brightness dazzled him, and it warmed his hands pleasantly as he held it. If only he could catch and remember that one fact about swans. It was something Mr. Masataka had mentioned in a history lesson, he was almost sure. It was something that would fit in perfectly—something that promised to link together all the pieces of the puzzle.

He stared at the sword's glowing hilt. How could it contain the "key" to this mysterious swan? He looked carefully at the lacy designs one more time. There was only one symbol on the handle that seemed even vaguely familiar to him. It was a slender, graceful arrow that ran the length of the handle, pointing up toward the sharp tip of the blade. He wondered if it could be more than just a decoration. Directly at the end of the arrow was a strange pattern of six dots, linked by broken lines. They formed a kind of ragged cross shape. The more William looked at it, the more he was sure that he'd seen that pattern before. But where?

Did it have something to do with the history lesson? He jammed his fist into his forehead, trying to think. What was the lesson about—old Earth mythology, perhaps? Slowly, things began to come back to him. That was it! They had been studying certain customs of some of the old Earth civilizations. It was something about stars in the dark, night skies. People had imagined things about those stars once. They, like the pioneers aboard the Genesis, had used the stars for steering their ships. So many stars! So many that any single star was impossible to find in the great, speckled sky.

Yes—yes! He remembered, now. The old Earthmen had divided the stars into groups. Each group made up an imaginary sort of picture. There were dragons and bears, winged horses and lovely ladies. There were hunters— and there was a swan! Yes! One group of stars had represented a swan. Now he remembered that one, well. It was made up of six stars, in the shape of a flying swan—or the shape of a ragged cross! The name of the star-group was Cygnus.

Breathing hard from sudden excitement, he examined the dots at the tip of the arrow once more. "I've got it!" he exclaimed. "My gosh, I've solved the puzzle!"

It was as if a great, warm light had suddenly flooded his mind with comprehension. He imagined himself standing quietly in a place where he had never been before, a place where there was firm, damp soil beneath his feet. Huge trees whispered in the fragrant air, and high in the brilliant sky rode a great, yellow sun.

He was sure it wouldn't be much longer before all his dreams of planets came true. For it was just as Orion had said it would be. Everything was perfectly clear to him. He could see exactly what had to be done, and how he was to do it.

Chapter Nine

Cygnus

Maggie pressed herself tightly against a bulkhead. There were voices not far off, down the short hallway that ran between the engines and the locker room. Shouts and orders rang out, bouncing hollowly off the bare metal walls and floors of the main engineering deck. She was frightened. It was clear to her that the high, loud voices meant some sort of trouble nearby, and she did not want to be caught in the middle of it, especially since there was no way for her to hide the towel she had managed to take from the locker room. She suspected that the trouble was another puncture in the hull, for she could hear above the voices a shrill, piercing whistle that was unmistakably different from the whine of the generator turbines.

Peeking around the corner, she found the hallway empty, and wasted no time in flinging herself down it toward the main corridor, which ended in the ghost lock where William would be waiting for her. She was hot and damp with perspiration, for the air on the engineering decks was humid and muggy with steam, produced by the Genesis' water purification system. She was used to the dry atmosphere of the rest of the Genesis. The extra moisture, combined with the ship's steady loss of air, left her slow and tired. Still, she forced herself to hurry on. There was no time to waste.

But as she started down the dim corridor where she had left William, she was alarmed to find that he was nowhere to be seen. He must be hiding, she thought, and hurried toward the ghost lock anyway. Yet, as she came nearer and nearer, she still could not see him.

"William," she called softly, but there was no answer. She felt her blood ringing in her ears as she hesitated at the open airlock hatch. Where could he be? There were no hiding places here, where the cargo hull suddenly ended in the thick fire wall. Suddenly, she was terribly afraid for him.

"William!" she screamed. But there was still no answer. He had disappeared into thin air! Frantically, she looked around the airlock. William and the sword had disappeared without a trace. She was on the verge of calling for help when she happened to spy a piece of paper drifting several centimeters from the deck. Eagerly, she picked it up. There, in large, hurried letters, was a note from William.

"Dear Maggie," it read, "I have figured out the message. Please go to the observation cone and wait for me there. Bring the towel with you because I am leaving Starnight there behind the dehumidifier coil for safekeeping."

"Thank goodness!" Maggie breathed, as she stuffed the note into her pocket. She slammed the hatch of the ghost lock, and rushed headlong down the bleak corridor toward the nose of the ship.

William ran toward the sick bay as fast as he could. Already the lights in the corridors were dimming. Soon, visiting hours would be over for twelve hours, and he would be unable to see the captain at all. He would have to waste precious time waiting for the one piece of information he needed, in order to use Starnight. That could be disastrous, for there was no time left, now. The situation was critical. He had passed three hull-leaks on his way to the sick bay already. If the Genesis lost much more oxygen, her supplies would begin to fail and then . . . he did not want to think about what would happen after that.

At the sick bay door, he rang the bell for the second time that day. The young nurse appeared again.

"Excuse me, ma'am, but I have to see the captain right away. It's urgent," blurted William.

The nurse frowned, looking indignant and surprised. "I think you'd better wait here a moment," she said, and disappeared from view, leaving him standing in the corridor.

A few minutes later she returned. "All right," she said, "the captain wants to see you, but Dr. Curtis will not allow you to stay more than a minute or two."

She led William into the captain's room again. He was lying on the bed with his eyes closed.

"Here's William Murdock, sir," said the nurse. Captain Stone's eyes flickered open and he struggled up on his elbows.

"Oh, thank you, nurse," he said. He seemed tired. The little wrinkles around his eyes looked deeper than ever before, and his shoulders seemed to droop as if he were carrying something heavy. "What is it, William?" he asked.

"Sir, I hope you don't mind, but I have a question to ask you," said William, panting to catch his breath.

Captain Stone smiled slightly as he replied, "Of course. Ask away."

"Sir, are you familiar with the constellation Cygnus?"

"Certainly," answered the captain. "Why do you ask?"

"Well, it's kind of a long story, but I have to find Cygnus right away, sir." William tugged nervously at his damp hair. "And I knew that after all this time it wouldn't look like the star charts in our science books anymore. Well . . . I was wondering if you could point it out to me, or draw me a picture of it."

"Has this got something to do with your golden man and your fantastic sword?" asked Captain Stone, raising one eyebrow.

William was surprised. "You've read what I said at the hearing, then, sir?" he said.

"Yes, I have," was the reply.

William hesitated only a moment. "Yes, sir," he said. "It does."

The captain pursed his lips, looking more tired and worried than ever. Then he took a piece of paper and a pencil from his bedside table, and began sketching a map of the sky on it. As he worked, he spoke in a soft, deep voice. "Murdock," he said, "we've tried everything we know of to save this ship, and we are losing the battle. I've read your story, and something inside me makes me believe it. So do what you must. You may be our last hope of finding a safe harbor somewhere out there." He smiled so faintly that William almost missed it. "You are the last thing left for us to believe in."

He handed William the sketch of Cygnus. "The stars will be spinning around you, of course."

William gasped. How could Captain Stone have known that he planned to go out on the hull again?

"No, don't say anything. It's written all over your face. I know you will go outside the ship again," said the captain. "I can't tell exactly where you will find this constellation. But it will be easiest if you face the forward end of the ship. When it comes around to where you can see it, Cygnus will be about thirty degrees from the horizon of the Genesis' nose. Good luck, son."

"Thank you, sir," said William, his heart suddenly leaping. "Thank you." Then he turned and rushed out the door and down the corridor on his way to the observation cone.

Maggie was waiting for him when he got there, her round face pale in the cold starlight as she slowly drifted with Starnight in her arms. "You made it! I was worried," she whispered.

The observation cone was deathly silent.

"You got the towel," said William. "Good. I was hoping you had."

Maggie handed him the sword, wrapped like a baby in the towel. "Have you really figured out what the message means?" she asked.

"Yes," answered William, carefully unwrapping Starnight. "It's funny. The idea just came to me, and I'm positive it will work. I've been down talking to the captain about it. He gave me this." He handed her the piece of paper on which Captain Stone had sketched the constellation Cygnus.

"What's this?" Maggie asked, wrinkling her nose.

"It's a drawing of a certain group of stars—the same stars in this diagram here." Leaning forward, he showed her the odd dots and lines on the handle of the sword.

"But what does it mean?" she asked.

William breathed deeply, wondering how to explain

the long and winding paths of thought that had led him to run feverishly off to the captain, for a star chart. "Well, it's quite a story," he said at last. "I haven't got enough time to explain it very well now. The important thing is that Starnight and I are going to go out on the hull again. Right away."

Maggie's mouth dropped open. "Oh, William, you know how much trouble you'll get into, if they catch you again."

"It doesn't matter anymore," answered William, still breathless from all his hurrying. "This is the most important thing I'll ever do in my life. It's more important than just you or me, or the captain, or even the council. Because all of our lives depend on it. I have to take the risk. It's going to be worth it, believe me."

Maggie's lower lip trembled, and for a long moment William wondered if she were going to cry. Instead, she looked at him with sudden fire and demanded, "Let me go with you."

William closed his eyes tightly. His heart thumped like a drum. Somehow, deep inside, he had hoped she would ask to come. For though he did not like to think about it, he was frightened. Orion's warning kept playing in his head like a broken record. He needed her help to keep from backing out. "I don't know what's going to happen out there. It could be very dangerous," he whispered, opening his eyes again.

"If you fail, we're all going to die soon," Maggie said, quietly. "If I go outside, I may be able to help you. Who knows? And I can promise you one thing. I'm no sissy. I won't get in your way no matter what happens." Her blue eyes flashed with determination.

William was about to answer her, when a shrieking whistle suddenly interrupted their conversation. It was so loud that he clapped his hands to his ears. It was another hull puncture. He could not tell exactly where the hole was, but he knew that it was very nearby, for his head felt as if it might crack like an eggshell with the pressure change. He grabbed Maggie by the arm. "Come on! Let's get out of here!" he shouted.

She nodded bravely, her forehead wrinkled with pain.

It was not long before they reached the nearest airlock. They suited up hurriedly, afraid that the puncture in the observation cone would soon bring a squadron of engineers running. They hardly spoke as they adjusted the tabs and buckles on the suits which they had chosen. The only sounds were the everpresent sighing of the power plants several decks away, and the distant whine of air rushing out through the hole in the observation cone.

Within ten minutes, William was turning the hand-wheel on the inner hatch, sealing them into the small cubicle through which they would climb out into the darkness of space. Inside his pressure suit, William already felt detached from the outside world. He felt his suit inflate as the oxygen flowed out of the airlock. Just before he opened the outer hatch, he caught a glimpse of Maggie's face, dwarfed by her great helmet. She smiled broadly and gave him the thumbs-up signal, her teeth gleaming brightly in the harsh fluorescent light of the cubicle.

Carefully, they edged their way out onto the catwalk, taking the sword with them. Glancing around, William saw with horror that the ship had changed noticeably since his last excursion just a few short weeks before. Everywhere he looked small bright geysers of dust-filled air spurted out through the hull.

William hesitated a moment to let Maggie get used to the terrifying upside-down feeling of standing on the hull. Then, afraid to use his radio for fear of being discovered, he touched helmets with her so they could hear one another speak.

"How far do we have to go?" he heard her ask in a thin voice, distorted by the metal through which it traveled.

"That depends," he answered. "We might not have to go far at all. One way or another, I have to find the stars I'm looking for."

William looked out at the endless, black sky. Slowly and relentlessly, the stars spun about him as the Genesis turned on its axis. Where was Cygnus? His suit rustled eerily as he twisted, straining his eyes as ancient sailors must have done, to find one group of stars among all the clusters of light that dotted space.

He tried to remember the detailed chart that Captain Stone had drawn for him. What was he looking for? He fumbled at the chest pocket of his space suit. What had he done with the chart? A sudden, empty feeling seized him. The paper was not in his chest pocket. Maybe he had left it in one of his coverall pockets!

"Oh, no!" he cried.

Maggie must have caught a glimpse of his agonized face even behind his protective visor, for she leaned toward him to touch helmets again. "What's wrong?" she asked.

"It's the star chart," William moaned. "I can't find it. I'm afraid I left it in my coveralls. It's impossible to reach it unless I go back to the airlock and take off my suit!"

"Wait, wait," answered Maggie calmly, touching his shoulder. "*I* have the star chart. You gave it to me, remember?" She laughed lightly, a far away, comforting sound like water in a distant tunnel. Almost gaily, she reached into her own chest pocket and brought out the rumpled piece of paper.

William relaxed, grinning at his mistake. "I guess I'm

pretty nervous," he said. "Boy, it's a good thing you made me bring you along."

Carefully he took the paper from her, holding it up before him in the light of his helmet lamp. It would be hard to spot one small group of stars when there were so many others to confuse him.

William studied the sky. He had never felt so tiny and unimportant before. The dark dome of space extended forever in all directions, a cool and unbeatable opponent for any who chose to go against its natural rules.

He kept his eyes about thirty degrees above the dully gleaming hull, watching as the stars traveled slowly above. Beside him, Maggie stood in silence, hardly moving as she, too, gazed at the scene around them.

Before long, William spied a constellation which seemed to fit Captain Stone's drawing. Carefully, he compared the stars to the chart in his hand. There was no question. He had found the constellation Cygnus. All the world moved as smoothly and slowly as melted butter while he unsheathed the mighty sword and raised it over his head. The stars seemed to hold their breaths for him. He felt the slight pressure of Maggie's hand as she patted him on the back and then stepped out of his way. William rested the sword's glowing hilt on his shoulder. He could see forever as he sighted along Starnight's graceful blade, then slowly pointed its tip at Cygnus. With strength he never knew he had before, he kept the great sword moving with the stars.

Nothing happened. William felt his heart begin to thump like an old and tired frog in his chest. He wouldn't think of failing. He wouldn't!

But just then Starnight began to vibrate softly. He watched it with curiosity, overwhelmed at the power he felt surging through it. Its pulsing light changed from soft orange to a bright yellow-white as the vibration steadily increased. William no longer had to guide the sword's tip along the arc of the constellation's path. Starnight guided itself, as if it were linked to Cygnus by some invisible chain.

The vibration, steady and soft, was very penetrating. It shook him until he felt as if his veins were thin, blue wires flowing with electricity. He felt strange, dizzy and suddenly drowsy as if he stood on the edge of a long, deep sleep. Clouds of glowing mist rolled before his eyes. Suddenly, a piercing stream of red light shot out of Starnight's tip. The sword jerked back at him, hitting him hard, and the clouds of mist blew away . . . but not quite soon enough. Before he could stop himself, his magnetic shoes broke away from the hull. Like a rocket gone wild, he fell and fell and fell away from the Genesis! Helplessly he tumbled into space.

"Maggie!" he screamed. He watched as she moved her arms frantically, unable to help him in any way. Both she and the Genesis grew smaller and smaller as he slipped away from them. In despair, he remembered that he had not clipped his safety line to the catwalk!

"Help me!" he cried. "What should I do?" But there was no one to hear him. He was very much alone. Terrified, he began to cry.

Then, through his tears, a small, firm voice came from inside him. "Don't be such a baby," it said. "Brave adventurer indeed! You're certainly not acting like one." William knew it was true. He sniffed and grew quiet. Crying wouldn't help him, but calming down would. He took a few deep breaths. "Heart, slow down," he said aloud. "The faster you beat, the more air I use."

When his heart had slowed down and his breathing was more normal, he noticed that Starnight, too, had been flung away from the ship and was drifting along a meter or so away from him. "Now look what you've gotten us into," he said, trying to make himself laugh. "When the rescue boats come, the old chief councilman will have me weeding the vegetables forever." But in the back of his mind he was afraid there would be no rescue boats. They wouldn't know where to begin the search for him. He shivered. They had no way of knowing where he was.

He looked over at Starnight. It had taken on its usual orangish glow again, and was tumbling serenely through space as if nothing had ever happened. He remembered the vibrations, the flash of red light, the strange mist that had filled his head just before he'd lost his balance. What did it all mean?

He wished that he could somehow catch hold of Starnight, bring it close, and examine it for some kind of clue. But there was no way he could change the direction of his drift, for there was nothing for him to push against or hold onto. He closed his eyes tightly. He might drift in space forever with no destination, the bright sword spinning along beside him. They might find him someday by chance, a withered corpse in a space suit. He shook his head and blinked. No good thinking things like that.

He switched his helmet radio on, hoping that he might be able to contact the ship, but he received no answers to his calls for help. Finally, hoping that the Genesis could hear him and home in on his signal, he began to sing—a happy little song that he had learned in school, a song about the great day when the ship would reach Earth II. It made him feel better.

He did not know how long he had been tumbling through the darkness, when he noticed a star that seemed different from the rest. It was difficult for him to be sure, but he fancied that the star was moving. After watching it closely for some time, he was certain. It *was*

85

moving. Not only that, but it seemed to be growing larger and brighter! He held his breath, hoping at first that it might be a rescue party from the Genesis. But as the spot of light grew nearer, he began to wonder. A rescue boat would be searching the sky for him with its powerful, bluewhite beams. But this object seemed too small and soft, and gave off a subdued, yellowish glow. Whatever it might be, it was coming toward him very quickly—faster than anything he had ever seen before.

He watched—half fascinated, half afraid—as the strange light grew larger and larger. "Oh, Starnight," he whispered, "if only I could catch you. Then maybe I would have a fighting chance!"

In a few seconds, the light was much closer, and he could see that it was not the smooth, round ball that it had appeared to be at first. He wished that he could rub his eyes to make sure that he wasn't just imagining it. The light looked almost like a huge bird of some sort, glowing softly as it sped through the darkness toward him.

Closer and closer it came until at last William was sure. *It was a huge, golden swan!* Its long neck waved gracefully as it approached with its wings neatly folded back along its sleek body.

All at once, a soft, powdery voice filled his helmet. "I am a friend of Orion's," it said. It was a light, girlish voice, happy and good, on the edge of laughter as bright as stardust. "Don't be so frightened. I've only come because you called me."

William stared, too overcome with astonishment to answer.

Chapter Ten

Riding the Folds of Space

Thrusting out his arms and legs, William struggled to get a better look at the amazing swan. But no matter how hard he tried, he could not turn himself.

The gigantic, golden creature moved closer to him until he could see her individual feathers and her clear, yellow eyes. Around her sleek neck hung the only ornament she wore—a great, amber jewel on a fine chain. It glowed as powerfully as the swan herself.

Without warning, a ripple of delicate laughter filled his head. "Do I frighten you? Do I frighten you so much?" said the swan.

William could not answer. Excitement clouded his thinking.

"I give you my word," she coaxed. "I am a Watcher, and a friend of Orion's. I have come to help you."

William's heart slowed a little at that. "Orion sent you?" he asked.

"No," she replied softly. "*You* sent for me, with

Starnight. You have passed the second test and earned the help of the Watchers in your search for the stones."

For a moment, William was too thrilled to say anything. He could hardly believe what he had heard. "You mean everything is going to be all right—the Genesis is going to be saved?" he said at last.

Though her golden beak did not move, he had the feeling that she smiled. "No, William. Your ship is not safe yet. Remember what Orion told you. We can only help if you are willing to help, too."

"Yes," said William anxiously, "I remember. I'll do anything you say. Anything at all."

She cocked her sleek, shining head. "It will not be easy. It will not be easy, even with all the help the Watchers can give," she said. "But first things first. You must be very tired. Come. Let me take you on my back."

William realized that what the swan had said was true. He was tired. It was nighttime on the Genesis and he had not had his supper. The last few hours had been filled with tension and tremendous physical and mental battles. Suddenly the idea of resting securely on the swan's broad back was very inviting.

William felt a slight bump and realized that the swan had come up from below him. He found himself seated on her soft back, Starnight clutched tightly in his hand. Slowly, he pushed the sword into the huge leather sheath which hung below his shoulder.

"You may take off that cumbersome helmet," she said. "I have brought a bubble of air for you."

William hesitated at the thought of removing his helmet in the harsh, unforgiving depths of space. "Are you sure?" he asked uncertainly.

"You must trust me," said the shining bird. "Without trust we can never be friends, and without a bond of friendship, we will never succeed in saving your ship."

He thought for a moment. The swan felt large, warm and comforting. Her voice was kind and inviting and she gave him the same feeling that Orion had given him—a certainty that she would never harm him. He loosened the fastenings and lifted off his helmet.

Delighted, he drank in the air from the shining bubble that surrounded them. It was fresh and pure, different from any he had ever breathed before.

"And what next?" he asked eagerly.

"Now we have a journey to begin, and little time in which to complete it," she answered. "You must rest while we travel."

And before his weary eyes, the bright stars began to move—slowly at first, changing into streaks of light as they gained speed. His mind was so numb with confusion that he didn't even question it. He did not care where they were going, nor how she could travel so quickly. Resting his tired head on her downy neck, he fell fast asleep.

When he awoke several hours later, the stars had disappeared!

"Swan, where did the stars go?" he asked sleepily.

For answer he received only her bell-like laughter. "Cygnus. Call me Cygnus, after my constellation," she said.

"Cygnus, then. Where are the stars?" he repeated. He was more awake by now, and the darkness outside their shining bubble of air alarmed him.

"Do not be afraid," she answered. "The stars are still there, only we cannot see them. We are traveling the folds of space where the light of suns can not catch us."

William marveled silently. For though he could not see the stars, there were other sights to take their place. The void was a wonderful panorama of moving shapes and colors. They reminded him of the bright patterns he sometimes saw when he closed his eyes very tightly and watched the changing darkness.

"We are going to a particular planet—many light years away from your ship," said Cygnus.

"To a planet!" cried William. "Are you taking me to Earth II, then? Will I be the first colonist to see it?"

"Goodness, how inquisitive you are," she replied, laughing. "No, no. Earth II is not the place we want—not for *this* trip, anyway."

"But Earth II is the closest. You mean we are going beyond it?"

"Yes, in a way, though the word 'beyond' hasn't much meaning out here in space," she answered.

"But how can we go that far?" exclaimed William. "It would take years and years!"

"Yes. It would take your *ship* years," she answered, "but you forget. I am a creature of space. I know my way among the folds and can travel faster than the designers of the Genesis ever dreamed."

"I don't understand," said William, puzzled.

Again Cygnus laughed softly. "It is too hard for me to explain. Let's just say that I am—taking shortcuts, from one point to another."

For a while they journeyed on in silence. But William was too full of questions to stay quiet for long. "On this planet can I get the gleaming stones Orion talked about?"

"Perhaps, if luck is with you and you are strong enough," answered Cygnus gravely.

William was a little surprised. "Is there trouble of some kind ahead?"

Cygnus twisted her sleek head toward him, her clear eyes gleaming like topaz. "You do not know, do you?" she cried softly.

The tone of her voice sent shivers up his back. "No,"

he answered, suddenly feeling very small. "What are you talking about?"

He felt the great bird sigh beneath him. "You have had the misfortune of being discovered by the Unhappy One," she said. "Surely you have felt his presence?"

"I don't know," replied William thinking back. "But for the last few days, I've suspected that something was trying to sabotage my plans for saving the Genesis." Facts were beginning to fall into place now like the pieces of a jigsaw puzzle.

"Then you *have* felt him," she said. "Indeed, your plans *were* sabotaged, by a being with great skill. The Unhappy One delights in destroying the hopes and dreams of others."

"Who is this 'Unhappy One'?" asked William slowly, not sure he wanted to hear the answer.

For a moment, Cygnus was silent, and she seemed to look far off into the distance. "Once, far back in the dim and misty past, he was a Watcher, like the rest of us. But he was weak. He became dissatisfied with his life of service. His unhappiness made him listen to a voice that the rest of us had long ago refused to hear. And he became evil."

William looked out at the changing patterns of space. "But why should he care about me?" he asked. "I haven't given him any reason to hate me."

Cygnus laughed dryly. "Do not think that the world is guided by reason," she replied.

William shivered. "You mean he has no reasons for the things he does?" he asked.

"None at all," she replied. "It is his way to be unkind. He does not think about it."

"But I don't understand that. It's just not natural. Why, no human being would ever act like that. Humans always have reasons for the things they do, no matter how bad the reasons may be," exclaimed William.

"Ah," answered Cygnus, "but you cannot make the mistake of supposing that every creature thinks like a human being. It is really not very common in this universe to find creatures with reasons for everything."

"Oh," said William, fidgeting. "I—I guess I didn't know that." He gazed into space, feeling somehow empty and lost.

Cygnus was quiet for a long moment. Then she said softly, "Don't be hurt, William. Nothing has changed, really."

But he could not answer. He was still trying to get used to what she had said.

"Come," she said at last. She made a soft clicking noise with her beak and lifted her great wings a little. "Lie down upon my back and rest. I will tell you a story; it may help you."

When William had made himself comfortable among her soft feathers, she waved her slender neck gracefully. "Long ago," she began, "before he had set the great clock of the universe in motion, the Creator was alone in the darkness. 'I will build a world,' he thought, for it was the nature of him to build and create. 'I will make a vast world from the meaningless dust of the void. The world will be filled with all sorts of creatures. And I will make three forces to rule all of them. The first two forces will be called Good and Evil, and by their natures they will be opposed to each other and bent on each other's destruction. Their opposition will serve to keep the world in motion. But the other force I will fashion in my own image, and it will not be concerned with the other two forces. Its name will be Creativity, and it will give the world direction.'"

As Cygnus said this, the stars suddenly reappeared in

a magnificent blaze across the heavens. Awestricken, William felt as if he himself were witnessing the act of creation the swan had described. Yet he remembered that the return of stars must mean he and Cygnus had left the folds of space behind. He wondered if they were rushing toward a meeting with that strange creature, the Unhappy One.

Cygnus continued as if she had not even noticed the reappearance of the stars. "When he had finished building the world, the Creator stood back and admired his work. 'I have done a fine job,' he thought, as he added the finishing touch by breathing energy into the world, to set it in motion.

"After a time, each of the three great forces which he had created claimed certain of the other creatures as its own. There were some who came to follow the force of Good. Some followed Evil, and still others followed Creativity."

Cygnus stretched her wings proudly until her feathers sparkled. "Orion and I and the other Watchers are servants of Good."

"And the Unhappy One?" asked William.

"He is a servant of Evil," she answered. "It happened that while casting his powerful mind about space, he found you and set to work to keep you from succeeding in your goal of saving the Genesis."

A shiver ran up William's spine as he thought of the mysterious, terrible things that had happened after he had brought Starnight aboard the ship. "Did the Unhappy One make Captain Stone sick?" he asked.

"Yes," answered the great bird.

"But that's not fair," protested William. "The captain didn't have anything to do with it."

"The Unhappy One wished to stop you in any way he could. He did not care who he hurt in order to do it."

"I just don't understand. Why should he hate me so much?" said William.

Cygnus answered firmly. "You must realize that he does not hate you; he feels no anger. He is simply wicked."

William shook his head. "It's too awful to imagine," he said. He ran his fingers through his hair. "He'll do everything he can to stop me from getting those special stones, won't he?"

"I'm afraid so," she answered sympathetically.

William bit his lip at her words. After a moment's thought he asked, "I won't have to face him alone, will I?"

Cygnus' answer was clear and firm. "Both my sword Starnight and I will be at your service. But it is well to remember that none of us can stop the Unhappy One singlehandedly."

"We'll stop him together, then," said William determinedly, patting Starnight's hilt. "We have to."

On and on they rushed in black and abysmal voids, past suns that spewed forth fire and light, through clouds of shimmering dust.

Finally, William made out a sparkling, greenish sphere looming in the distance. "Is that the planet?" he asked, fear and excitement suddenly bubbling through his veins.

"Yes," answered Cygnus, turning to look at him, her eyes bright. "You have never been on a planet before, have you?"

"No, this will be the first time," answered William, barely able to contain himself.

Cygnus laughed as if amazed. "How strange," she said. "Well, at least the atmosphere will suit you. It's a great deal like the inside of your ship. Still, I wonder. Do you know about seasons, and about day and night?"

"Well, sort of," he answered. "I've read about them. I know what causes them."

"We are going to a cave where the stones can be found," she continued. "It is summer now in the area of the cave. But it is also night, and will be, for some time—five or six hours. We must not try to fight the Unhappy One in the darkness. Your eyes are not made for it. So we will hide until morning."

"But won't the Unhappy One find us anyway?" William protested. "He *is* very powerful."

"Yes, but even *his* power is limited," answered Cygnus. "He is better at seeing things that are far away than he is at seeing things nearby. If we are careful, he will not find us."

Before long, they were rushing down through the atmosphere, a delicate envelope of brightest blue that shielded the planet from the fierce rays of the nearby sun. Cygnus rushed swiftly toward the distant line of darkness on the side of the planet opposite its star. As they approached the surface, William took great gulps of the fragrant, smooth air which ran like violet silk into his lungs. Below him spread mountains, plains, and canyons. Out near the horizon lay a huge body of water, as blue as the clear sky itself. "That must be an ocean," he whispered in excitement. "A real ocean on a real planet!"

In a moment, they came to rest on a dark, tree-covered hill. He heard Cygnus' gentle laughter behind him like the splash of water on stones. "Look around," she urged.

He dismounted and stood very still in the night. The darkness was filled with quiet sounds. Some of them he recognized from the Earth chamber—the chirping of insects in rhythm with some invisible clock, and the sleepy noises of birds. But he had never before heard the gurgling of water in the bed of a rocky stream, or the rush of warm wind in the boughs of evergreens. The world seemed filled with magic.

"Look at the stars," Cygnus whispered from behind him. Up in the cloudless sky, set like jewels in the crown of the Creator, millions of stars rose twinkling. Some were bright, some were faint, some formed great bands and clusters of light. "They're beautiful!" said William softly. "Beautiful!" He hefted Starnight in his hands, relishing its great weight in the planet's gravity. He felt strong and happy. He felt like a young animal in the forest, knowing he belonged there as he had never known anything before.

After William had stared at the night for a few minutes longer, Cygnus suggested that he cut himself some evergreen branches for a bed while she looked for his dinner.

"Thank you," said William, suddenly realizing that he had not eaten for what seemed ages.

After watching Cygnus disappear into the bushes, he raised Starnight as if it were an ax and trimmed a few of the lower branches from a nearby evergreen. The sweet odor of fresh pitch swept over him in a delicious wave. He thought longingly of Maggie and his parents back on the ship. If only they could know the wonder of a real planet. If he could beat the Unhappy One, before space sucked the last bit of life-giving oxygen from the Genesis, then maybe his dreams would come true.

As he was arranging the branches in a soft heap, Cygnus emerged from the darkness with a round, purple ball in her beak. "I think you will like this," she said after she had dropped it into William's outstretched hands. "I'm sure you have never tasted anything like it. This fruit grows only on this planet."

"Thank you," said William, smiling. He took a small bite while Cygnus looked on with a knowing twinkle in her eyes.

At once his mouth was filled with the most wonderful taste he could ever have imagined.

Cygnus watched him as he hungrily finished the fruit. "Human beings are handsome creatures," she said, cocking her head and blinking at him.

William smiled and laughed. "Not nearly as handsome as you Watchers," he replied. "Why, you and Orion are two of the most beautiful creatures I have ever seen."

"Ah, but the truth of that is hard to measure," said the swan. "For Orion and I have no bodies like yours. We are made up mostly of pure energy, and can take whatever shape we please—though we always glow. Our glowing is a sign that we are alive, you know."

William shook his head, amazed. "You mean, you're not really a swan?" he asked.

"No, indeed." Cygnus' eyes were sparkling.

"Well, what do you *really* look like then?" William wrinkled his nose.

"Oh, it is hard to describe. A small and misty star, perhaps, when my energy is free. But, do you see this?" She pointed with her beak at the amber stone that hung around her neck.

William nodded.

"This is like a little container. It is the place where most of me is concentrated, though some of me is in Starnight, too. Orion has a wide, golden belt which serves him the same way."

"That's amazing," exclaimed William. "And you never take the necklace off?"

"No, never," she answered. "I will wear it until the day I die."

The stars winked in the sky above as he stretched himself comfortably on his evergreen bed, resting his head on Cygnus' fluffy back.

"I have only one more question now," he said as he stared drowsily into the night. "You've been kind to me. You and the other Watchers are helping me to save the Genesis. But why?"

Cygnus was silent for a long moment. A warm breeze shushed among the tall trees as she answered. "It was Orion who found you. He watched your ship for a long time—until he discovered where you came from. Ah, you are the seed of a lonely little planet that whirled around a forgotten star. And long ago that little planet died, in a collision with a comet. You see, the Genesis contains all that is left of your kind."

William blinked. "The Earth is gone?" he whispered unsteadily.

"I am sorry," replied Cygnus.

The rush of his own blood filled his ears with thunder as he listened.

"It is not our way to let an entire race perish in the cold of space. Yet these are dark times. We could not afford to save you if it could be proven that you were evil. So we devised the test," continued the great swan.

She smiled gently at something he could not quite understand. "The results were better than we dared to hope," she said. "Though you proved to us that your race was capable of goodness, you showed us something far more important in the process."

"What was that?" asked William in a small voice.

"Think a moment," she replied. "The Creator made *three* forces. Creatures of simple Good and Evil are common in this universe of ours. But creatures of the third kind..."

Her voice trailed off into silence, leaving only the night sounds once more.

William drew a deep breath and let it out slowly.

"Sure," he said. "I should have guessed it from the first. We're the ones who create. The ones he made in his own image!"

Cygnus nodded her shining head.

It was a long time before William fell asleep.

Chapter Eleven

The Cave of Light

The sky was already warm and golden with the light of the rising sun when something made William awaken with a jump. Blinking, he groped for Starnight where it lay in its leather sheath beside him.

"What happened?" he mumbled, trying to clear the cobwebs of sleep away. Something had made him wake up—a noise perhaps. Yet he could not quite remember what it was.

"Shhh. Don't move." It was Cygnus, several feet away, peering over the long grass toward something William couldn't see. "He's come, just as I feared."

William's fingers tightened on the hilt of the sword. "The Unhappy One?" He shivered.

But there was no need for Cygnus to answer, for just then the very ground seemed to tremble with a distant roar of terrible laughter. Then a rumbling voice filled the air with a strange and vulgar language. And though William had never heard the language before, the words seemed to somehow march into his brain like angry soldiers and force him to understand.

"By the fires of space, come and get me, fools!" roared the voice. There was another roll of hideous laughter. "I dare you to try, you sniveling cockroaches. I am greater than an army of scum like you!"

William began to shake. Each word struck in his heart like a tiny blade of ice. But Cygnus laid her wing upon his hand and said calmly, "You must have the strength to overcome his lies."

William thought of the Genesis and of his family and friends. He plucked up his courage. "What does this cave look like?" he asked. "Is there a rear entrance?"

"Aaaah!" cried Cygnus, joyfully. "I knew you were strong." Pointing eagerly with her beak she continued, "The cave is just on the other side of this little hill. But I cannot say for certain whether or not there is a rear entrance. Come. We can see the cave from here." And crouching low in the fragrant grass, they crept toward the rim of the hill.

William clutched the heavy sword as he peered across the meadow toward the deep and shadowy cave. Before the entrance towered a huge, shapeless creature. The mere sight of the monster made him feel as if an invisible arm had pierced him with a knife made from frozen steel.

The Unhappy One was gigantic. He sat squarely before the cave entrance shouting a disgusting stream of obscenities. He had no eyes that William could see, nor any arms or legs. He sat immobile, a mountain of greenish slime with only one feature, a huge, cavernous mouth which gaped in William's direction. The mouth was blacker than deepest space—so black that the gaily dancing beams of the yellow sun were swallowed up by it. It was as if the monster's jaws sucked in and ate all light that came near, snuffing it into darkest night. A sudden

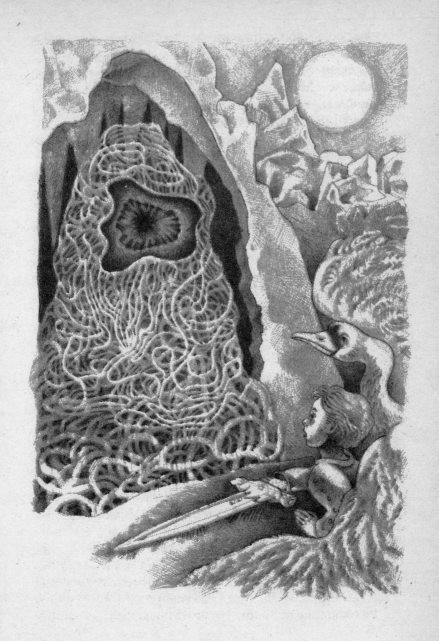

fear of falling into that hole seized William and made his heart cry, "Run! Run!" But he stayed where he was, listening to a stronger voice inside him, a voice that asked what would become of Maggie, of his mother and father, and of the rest of those aboard the Genesis if he could not outwit the Unhappy One.

William hunched down in the grass and inched backward to where Cygnus waited silently.

He chewed softly at his lip. "You said the Unhappy One has no reasons for the things he does," William mused. "Can he think? Can he reason at all?"

Cygnus cocked her head slightly on her slender neck and looked at him quizzically. After a long pause she answered, "No . . . no, as a matter of fact, I don't think he *can* reason. Not the way humans do anyway. I mean, he can't think ahead. He acts only on the moment."

William grinned. "That's what I'd hoped," he said. "He's not very smart—just strong. It won't take a very complicated plan to catch him off guard."

Cygnus' golden face seemed to light up at the idea. "Ah, Maker be praised. Orion has chosen very well!" she cried.

"I sure hope so," mumbled William, his cheeks burning. "Here—I'll explain my idea to you . . ."

A few moments later he was creeping through the long grass toward the rocky hillside at the monster's flank. He would circle the hill if he had to, in order to find a second entrance to the cave. He tried not to think of what he would have to do if his search was fruitless.

The Unhappy One's shouts and laughter rang like rockets in his ears as he reached the place where the grass began to thin out and the ground became rocky and treacherous. William prayed silently that his feet would be swift and sure on his winding search across the hillside. One slip, one noise of a falling pebble, and he would be finished. Warily, he glanced back over his shoulder. Apparently the Unhappy One had not yet discovered him.

He ducked behind a boulder and scanned the tumble of rocks above. Perspiration streamed down his face in the hot sun. The hillside was a confusing jumble of light and shadow that made it hard to tell clefts in the rock from patches of shade.

Slowly he worked his way across the boulders, stopping now and then to take another look above him for possible openings in the ground. The sun was well up in the sky by now and heat was beginning to rise from the rocks in tremendous waves that distorted the hillside and made him dizzy. But he kept at it, pushed on by the Unhappy One's terrible laughter and the thought of the Genesis marooned somewhere out there in space.

Then, as he looked up over the boulders one more time, he fancied he saw a shadow that was darker than a shadow ought to be.

Quietly, he climbed across the heaps of sharp rocks until he reached the spot.

"Oh, thank goodness!" he whispered, dropping to his hands and knees before the opening. From a small hole in the ground came a steady, cold wind. William stuck his head into the stony darkness. "This has to be it," he said, patting Starnight's hilt. "What luck!"

There was no time to waste. Taking a small flashlight from the thigh pocket of his space suit, he crawled into the tunnel. The passageway was very narrow and dark. Sometimes the roof was so low that he had to wiggle along on his stomach, hoping for the best. The walls were dank and clammy, covered here and there with slimy growths of fungi.

It seemed as if he had crawled for hours through the

inhospitable tunnel, when at last he thought he saw a glimmer of brightness ahead. He lay still and flicked off his flashlight. Sure enough, very dimly in the distance he could see that his passageway ended in an intersection with another tunnel. The light could mean that he was near the main cave.

Eagerly he scrambled on until he came to the other tunnel, which was large enough for him to stand up in. Looking both ways, he decided to go in the direction from which the light seemed to be coming.

He had trotted along for several meters when the tunnel suddenly veered to the left and opened into a large chamber where sunlight poured down through a hole in the ceiling. William gritted his teeth with impatience and disappointment. It wasn't the main cave after all. He had followed a false lead!

He looked about, trying to decide which way to go. He was still fairly certain that he was on the right track, for he could hear the Unhappy One's yelps and howls echoing in the distance ahead of him. Across the chamber, he saw a dark opening in the wall where the tunnel continued. Eagerly, he trotted into it.

Once again he had to rely on the pale beam of his little flashlight to guide him. In his hurry, he stumbled and fell once or twice, then lay breathlessly listening. Had the monster heard him? No, for the chilling laughter continued far away as if nothing had happened. Once he surprised a nest of large, white spiders. They ran up the tunnel walls and sat clicking their mandibles at him as he passed, so frightened and disgusted that he could hardly keep from screaming.

Without warning, the tunnel turned sharply and the Unhappy One's tremendous voice became very clear. William saw plainly that the passageway had ended and that there was light ahead. Warily, he switched off the flashlight and crawled on his stomach toward the bright patch ahead.

At last he reached the end of the tunnel and peeked out. He gasped! Directly below him was a sheer drop of at least fifteen meters. The end of his passageway came out far up on one of the walls of the main cave. Below and to his right stood the Unhappy One, blocking the front entrance.

William drew his head back in and shuddered at the sound of the monster's bellowing and cursing. "I can't go out there. I can't!" he thought desperately. "The Unhappy One will finish me for good if I don't fall off the wall first." He covered his face with his hands.

But just then he heard Cygnus' clear voice, like a silver trumpet, from outside.

"The Watchers have sent me with a warning."

"Don't bother me, you muddle-headed mound of feathers," was the thunderous response.

"Listen well, Evil One," said Cygnus. "It is the opinion of the Watchers that your shadow of misery can be allowed to grow no longer. Steps will be taken to curb you."

William's head resounded with the monster's laughter. "Watchers! Don't make me laugh so hard."

Slowly, William's courage began to return. After all, his plan was working almost perfectly. He had found a rear entrance and now Cygnus was acting as a decoy to keep the monster's attention. Once again he peeked out.

This time he noticed something that fairly made his heart skip a beat. Here and there in bright streaks and veins, the walls of the cavern danced with colors. The very stones seemed afire with the beams of some hidden star. In places, the walls moved with bright, colored light

107

as if they lay deep beneath an enchanted sea. There could be no mistake. Gleaming stones, Orion had said. The cave was full of them!

"Do not underestimate us," he heard Cygnus call.

She was answered with more laughter—laughter as cold and wild as a norther gale.

William knew that he hadn't much time. He must climb down to the nearest vein, collect some of the stones, and then hurry back out the rear entrance before the Unhappy One discovered him. Carefully, he lowered himself out onto the wall. His feet slipped precariously on the moist, slimy rocks. Slowly, painfully, he made his way toward the bright vein. Sweat poured down his face into his eyes and mouth. His fingers slipped and bled as he strained for good handholds. Every second he was certain he would crash to his death on the boulders below.

Dimly, he heard the Unhappy One shout a retort to Cygnus' threat. "Ha! How could I underestimate you? You pack of fools! Don't you think I know that there's no way you can hurt a living creature?"

Cygnus' voice came thinly from beyond the entrance. "Monster, you have been warned. Change your ways or be destroyed," she said calmly.

William barely heard her in his excitement. He had reached the gleaming stones and was trying to pry some loose with his hands. But it was no use. He needed something stronger to use as a tool. "Starnight!" he thought, and locating a better handhold, he drew the sword out and began to tap its hilt against the stones. Slowly, he loosened a few and stuffed them into his pockets. More and more came loose in his bleeding hand until at last his pockets would hold no more. Smiling, he began to think of climbing back up the wall.

The evil hiss of the Unhappy One's dry laughter

echoed through the cavern. "Away with you, slime. I am tired of your squawking. You bore me."

"Don't be too hasty!" Cygnus' voice had an edge of tension in it.

Time was running out. William had to hurry. He lifted Starnight to slip it back into its sheath. Then, as if in a nightmare, the worst possible thing happened. The great sword missed the sheath and tumbled clattering and echoing down to the cavern floor!

He felt the cave tremble as the Unhappy One shifted his great weight. "What was that? I heard something!" the monster bellowed.

William thought faster than he would have dreamed possible. There were things he had to remember—things he had to do. First, he had to get hold of the sword. That was the most important. Even as he struggled down the rocks toward Starnight, he was thinking. There was a strong echo in the cave. He could use that. And the Unhappy One was very poor at finding things that were near him. That was another thing to remember.

"It was nothing! I made that noise!" Cygnus shouted. But it was too late.

"Aaar..." roared the Unhappy One, and the ground shook. "You tricked me! That little cockroach friend of yours... Aaar! I'll kill you!"

William reached the sword and grabbed it up just as the Unhappy One turned to face the inside of the cavern. "Kill! Kill!" howled the monster.

William shivered for a moment, trying to keep his thoughts from running away in a black river of confusion. He knew that although his idea went against every instinct, it was his only chance.

"Hey!" he shouted as loudly as he could. His voice bounced off the rocks in perfect choruses. "Bet you can't catch me... can't catch me... can't catch me..."

Before the last echo had died away, William was hidden behind a boulder only meters away from the Unhappy One. "Where are you?" shrieked the monster. "Come out! All of you, or I'll blast you into space!"

William's heart thumped wildly. The plan was working! "Naa-naa-nanny goat!" he shouted. "You couldn't catch a flea . . . catch a flea . . . catch a flea . . ."

"Aaar! Aaar! I'll blast you!"

All at once streams of white fire rocketed out of the monster's devilish mouth. A boulder across the cave exploded into tiny pieces. A chunk fell down from the ceiling. A stalactite stuck, quivering like a colossal spear, between two rocks. The monster roared insanely, shooting forth more streams of fire.

William screamed as a piece of the wall above came tumbling down toward him. Covering his face with his arm, he threw himself behind a boulder, but not before a sharp splinter of rock smashed into his knee, ripping a deep, red gash through his space suit. "Cygnus! Help me! Help me!" he cried, as another shower of stone rained down.

"Come out! Come out! I'll tear you to pieces!" roared the monster.

"I'm afraid not." Cygnus' smooth, clear voice sliced the Unhappy One's ravings like a knife. For a moment the cave was silent except for the patter of loose pebbles rolling down new heaps of rubble.

The monster turned as if thunderstruck and hesitated a moment. Cygnus hovered in mid-air, her wings spread full and gleaming.

Then, with a tremendous roll of laughter, the Unhappy One seemed to fix on her at last, and the firing began again. But Cygnus was nimble, taunting him by gracefully dodging his missiles.

110

"Run, William! Get out!" she cried down to him.

"I'm trying!" William screamed. But his wounded leg refused to bear any weight. Three times he toppled into the rocks without getting anywhere.

"Run! I don't know . . . how much longer . . . I can hold out!"

William looked up in horror. Cygnus appeared to be tiring. The bolts of fire were missing her by less and less each time.

Tears ran down his dusty face as he finally stood upright, using Starnight for a crutch. The monster filled the whole entrance. He could not see any way to get past. Another blast of splintered rock came down and he held up an arm to shield his head.

"Ah, ha ha ha!" cried the Unhappy One. "I am beating you."

Cygnus voice was weak as she dodged one more time. "The sword. Use the sword!"

She plunged straight at the monster. For a second, the thing drew back in surprise. In a flash William realized what she was doing. She was giving him a chance—the one opening he needed to use Starnight. Raising the sword, he used his good leg and the last bit of strength he had to launch himself into the Unhappy One's slimy flesh.

He felt the monster quiver as Starnight's savage tip penetrated the shapeless body. He heard a terrible roar. And from the corner of his eye, he thought he saw something that looked like a small and misty star. Then darkness closed over him and he knew no more.

William lay with his eyes closed for a long while after he had come to. He heard the distant, cool rhythm of water trickling into a pool somewhere far back in the cave. He lay quietly, aware of the hot pounding in his injured knee, the lumpy sharpness of the rocks upon which he had fallen, and the dank, musty odor of wet earth.

He opened his eyes. He lay on his back near one of the cave walls, his head propped painfully on a sharp stone. Streaks of soft, golden light flowed from the entrance through dust motes raised by the Unhappy One's fire blasts. Before him, the monster lay in a lifeless heap, a great stream of green ichor running down its slimy hulk into a puddle among the boulders.

William felt the smooth firmness of Starnight's hilt still clutched in his right hand. He closed his eyes briefly, savoring a bit of pride in the fact that he had kept hold of his sword all through the battle. But when he opened his eyes again and looked down, he could not believe what he saw. Starnight's light had gone out! William blinked. A ray of sun glinted dully on the sleek, dark sword. The magical brightness was gone. Starnight's intricately carved blade was black as tarnished silver, its tip smeared with the Unhappy One's green blood.

Still somewhat dazed, William sat up painfully and examined his injured leg. His knee felt hot and swollen. Blood had flowed over the tear in his space suit and welled into a little pool among the pebbles. Taking out his handkerchief, he bandaged the wound as well as he was able, though he couldn't bear to tie the cloth tightly enough to stop the bleeding completely. Leaning on Starnight, he stood up shakily, keeping his weight on his good leg.

"Cygnus!" he called weakly, half choked by the dust which had still not settled. "Where are you?"

There was no answer but the rattle of loose pebbles set rolling by his echoing voice.

"Cygnus!" William gazed about the dim cave. His shining swan was nowhere to be seen. "She wouldn't just leave me here," he shivered, suddenly afraid. He remembered the last few moments of the battle. She *had* been weakening.

He took out his flashlight. The lens was cracked but the little bulb still worked. He shone it around the cave floor without any luck. Cygnus just wasn't there. He was about to give up and look outside when the beam suddenly reflected against something that lay on the ground. William looked closer. What he saw made him cry out in anguish. It was the amber jewel that Cygnus had always worn on the chain around her neck. It was as dark and cold as Starnight! He remembered what the lovely swan had told him the night before—that *she would wear the stone until the day she died*.

Just then, he felt the firm pressure of a large, warm hand on his shoulder. "Do not weep, little lion," said a quiet voice. He knew who it was before he turned to look.

"Oh, Orion," he sobbed. "She's dead, isn't she?"

Orion answered by gathering him softly into his great arms. The tarnished sword hung loosely, forgotten, in William's pale hand, as he cried for Cygnus.

With a whoosh like wind itself, Orion swept him out of the cave into the bright sunlight of midday summer. The giant set him gently in the cool, tall grass and kneeled to examine William's leg. "Bad," he said, shaking his head. He reached into his tunic and brought out a bottle filled with rich, orange liquid. He poured it carefully onto the wound. In a moment, the pain disappeared and William's knee felt cool, as if it had been steeped in mint or cold water.

"You've broken the bone," said Orion. "I am sorry I cannot heal you, but at least the ointment should take away the pain for a while."

William wiped his eyes. "Thank you," he said. "It already feels better."

"Well," said Orion with a deep sigh, "I wish there were

an ointment for the pain in your heart. I wish there were one for mine. The death of a great enemy pales before the death of a great friend."

William nodded woodenly. "She saved my life. She saved my life," was all he could say.

Wind whispered in the tall trees as Orion got to his feet. "Take up your sword, little lion, for it is yours now. Soon its light will come back. It's power will return, and you will be its new master for as long as you live."

Reaching out, William grasped the dark sword by its handle. It was cold and heavy, as cheerless as empty space. "Mine? But it was a part of Cygnus. I could never feel it was really mine."

"Things will not always be as they are today. Keep Starnight as a token of our esteem. You will see."

William stared emptily at the long blade. "So this is what it was all coming to," he murmured. "It's all over with now. I have the stones. And Cygnus is dead."

Orion looked out across the meadow, a strange mist across his eyes as if they were focused on something that William might never see. "Yes," he answered. "Cygnus is dead. But so is the Unhappy One."

From far across the field, the sad, sweet call of a bird floated. William sat without moving or thinking, like the stump of a tree hit by lightning.

"We had hoped for a happier ending. We only wished to help," said Orion quietly.

William looked up. "Well, you told me from the first that it wouldn't be easy." He shuddered. "Not easy at all." He suddenly felt very cold and tired. He began to shiver.

Orion frowned and his eyes darkened. "That is a bad wound. You are not well."

"I'm okay . . ." William began.

But the giant held up one broad-palmed hand. "My friend, say no more, for time is short. You have killed the

Unhappy One, and we can never repay you for it. Yet, we wish to show our gratitude somehow. We ask you to accept three more gifts from us. The first you earned long ago, at the very beginning of your adventure." As he spoke, Orion reached into the deep folds of his tunic again and brought out a tiny golden cup and a small, matching hourglass, both threaded on a fine chain.

"Take these," he said, stooping to drop the chain over William's head. "Guard them with your life, for without them the stones are useless to you."

William touched the chain carefully. "What are they?" he asked.

"Listen well," answered Orion. "Grind the glowing stones to powder. When you have made the powder, get some water and a long, slender container made of heavy metal—lead will do.

"Listen closely. This you must remember above all else. Calculate the distance to your destination by finding out how many turns of the hourglass it would take you to reach your planet at the speed of light. For every turn of the hourglass, use one cupful of powder and two cupfuls of water. Mix them in the metal container. Aim the open end of the container exactly 180 degrees away from your destination. There must be nothing between the open end and the clear stars."

As Orion spoke, a warm, stiff breeze was rising. The tops of the trees began to sway, and the meadow grass rattled like bones.

The golden giant looked away toward the far horizon, his brow still lined with concern. "I must go soon," he said quickly.

William, too, sensed something in the air—a kind of urgency that made his heart beat fast. He looked questioningly at Orion.

"Before we say good-bye, I offer you the second gift,"

said the giant. Taking an arrow from his quiver, he mounted it to his fantastic bow. "Little lion, for our second offering may you be forever marked with the sign of our friendship—the greatest gift of all." Slowly, he reached down and touched William's hand with the tip of the great arrow.

He looked up at Orion once more, but it was as if a thin fog hung between them. He began to feel weak and dizzy. He could not sit up anymore, and he fell back toward the grass. "Orion!" he cried, as he slipped into unconsciousness. "Don't go!"

"Good-bye, friend. And now, our third gift—a safe journey home," was the whispered answer.

Then all was dark as he spun toward the ground.

Momentarily, he had a dream of the cold stars, hung in their velvet sky.

Chapter Twelve

A Strange Journey

William drifted in a dizzying mist, waiting and waiting to hit the ground as he fell backward. "Orion!" he cried. But there was no answer. Then he blinked and suddenly realized that in fact he was lying on the carpeted floor of the Genesis' bridge!

For a long moment, there were no sounds but the soft hums and clicks of the navigation instruments. The officers stared in astonishment. William himself was too amazed to speak in those first seconds as he came to realize that Orion, the planet, and the cave were gone, and that somehow he had crossed the vast sea of space in what seemed like a matter of seconds. He was home. Yet there were the cup and the hourglass suspended on their chain about his neck; he could feel the lumpy firmness of the stones in his pockets; and in one hand he clutched Starnight, which was already beginning to glow again. He looked in silence at the back of his left hand, which tingled slightly. There, glowing like a miniature star, was a twinkle of white light, just in the spot where Orion had tapped him with the arrow.

Then, all at once, the bridge erupted with excited voices. He heard someone on the intercom, calling the captain to the bridge in a high pitched voice.

"William Murdock!" exclaimed the second officer, bending to help him sit up. "This is impossible. Just impossible. There's no way you could still be alive!"

"Oh, he's been hurt!" cried one of the laser operators, a young woman. "Get the doctor, someone."

But at that moment, Captain Stone burst through the door. "What the devil is going on?" he thundered.

"Why, it's that Murdock brat again!" squealed Councilman Zerski, who had followed the captain to the bridge. Then, spying William's bloody knee, he held his hand to his mouth and murmured, "Oh, my word."

"Captain Stone!" William cried. "You're well again!" He wanted to jump for joy, but instead he could only lean weakly against the second officer.

"Murdock! It's a miracle," cried the captain in return, striding vigorously to where William lay. "How can it be?"

"I'm certainly glad to see you feeling better, sir," grinned William.

"Better, aye—and have been since the day after we lost you." The captain squatted beside him, his forehead deeply creased as he looked at William's leg. "But what about yourself? What terrible thing has happened to you? Where have you been? And what in the world did this?" He nodded toward William's knee.

Suddenly William felt confused and lightheaded. Orion's potion seemed to be wearing off and his leg ached dully. His mouth was dry and he felt as if all the blood had rushed from his head. He could not say a word.

Someone brought him a glass of water.

Dimly he heard Zerski say, "What's taking the doctor so long?"

A moment later he felt a cool, soft hand on his forehead. When he opened his eyes, he found his mother and father gazing down at him.

Somewhere behind him, the second officer said, "The boy just appeared from nowhere. Everyone on the bridge saw it." There was a murmur of agreement from the rest of the crew.

"We're just glad to have him back," said Mr. Murdock, "questions or no questions."

Maggie was there, too. She picked up his left hand—the one with the faint spot of light set on it like a tiny diamond. "Look! Look!" she cried. "Oh, William. Where have you been?"

"Strange . . . strange," said the captain softly, shaking his head. "A miracle."

In a moment, William found his voice again and said, shakily, "Sir, none of that is important now. The thing is, I've succedded in getting a special fuel and a formula for using it. We can save the Genesis now."

A blazing light came slowly into the captain's eyes. The bridge erupted into a chaos of amazed exclamations. "Oh, good heaven above," he whispered.

A few hours later, William hobbled on crutches down the long corridor outside the sick bay.

Maggie walked close beside him, looking concerned. "Are you feeling better now?" she asked.

"Yes, a lot better," he answered, smiling. Actually, he was still feeling a bit groggy after his short and fitful sleep. But the ship's surgeon had put a bulky, plaster cast on his leg and, although it made walking difficult, it eased the pain in his knee tremendously.

"Well, that's good," said Maggie. "The captain's waiting for us in the central hull."

"What's left to be done?" asked William as they arrived at the elevator.

"Well, I'm not exactly sure. I know the captain has all the figures from the computer. He had the engineers put together a lead container and mount it outside the firewall. And I think the ship's chemists have already ground up the rocks. Oh, William! It's so exciting! The whole ship is standing by to strap into acceleration couches on a minute's notice."

William smiled as he limped into the elevator. "I'm glad you came and got me," he said. "I would have been very sad to wake up and find I'd missed it all."

"William! You know we wouldn't have let you miss it. Why, if it weren't for you, none of this would be happening."

The elevator stopped with a slight lurch and the doors slid open. William floated out into the corridor, crutches and all, with Maggie close behind him.

"Toward the firewall?" he asked, glancing up and down the long, dim hallway.

"That's right," Maggie answered.

William pushed gently against the floor with his crutches, as if he were a boatman poling a barge down a muddy canal, and off he flew.

"Nothing slows *you* down, does it?" laughed Maggie, trailing behind.

William chuckled. "I wouldn't say that," he called, thinking back to his terrible battle only hours before.

They had almost reached the firewall when Maggie tugged at his sleeve. "It's this last hatch to the right. Captain Stone should be waiting there."

Sure enough, as they slowed so that they could enter the chamber, Captain Stone stuck his head out the hatchway, looking for them. "Here you are at last!" he called, beaming. "We've all been waiting for you."

To William's surprise, there was a great cheer as they entered the chamber. A large group of his shipmates lay strapped into acceleration chairs, clapping and smiling.

He looked around. Among the waiting crowd were his parents, some of the officers from the bridge, and even the chief councilman!

"I—I don't know what to say," murmured William, looking at the deck, his face so hot that it seemed almost afire.

"Come," said Captain Stone, taking his arm and leading him through the rain of applause. They ducked through another hatch at the back of the chamber. The captain spun the handwheel.

"Here we are, Murdock," said Captain Stone. "Let me show you what we've been doing."

William turned to face the other bulkhead, which adjoined the firewall. A small window with thick, clear plastic set into it had been cut in the wall. Below the window was a panel of controls for operating a set of robot hands which were placed on the other side of the firewall. There were two acceleration couches on the deck near the controls.

He floated over to get a better look at what was on the other side of the window. Outside were three engineers putting the finishing touches on a metal stand with a long, lead container on top.

"Have you already measured the powder and water?" asked William, as he watched.

"Yes, they'll place the powder in the container just before they come back inside. The water's in that syringe attached to the stand. It's held there with a magnet. When we're ready to use it, we'll just grab it with the mechanical hands," answered the captain.

William felt Maggie tap him on the shoulder. "I thought you might like to have this, just for extra courage." She handed him his beautiful sword, its hilt sparkling where it stuck out of the sheath.

"Starnight!" he cried. "Gee, thanks, Maggie." He slipped the sheath over his shoulder.

"I'll have to go sit with the others now. But good luck. We'll be watching you on the video screen, so I won't have to miss too much," she said with a little smile.

"Thanks again, Maggie. You know I couldn't have done it without you."

William opened the hatch for her and she climbed through. He peeked out after her. The colonists sat eagerly before the large television screen, still strapped into their couches. It was obvious that the thinness of the air was already affecting some of them. There was the chief councilman, looking milkier and more frail than ever. There were the rest of the councilmen, some of them brave and easy in their chairs, some of them stiff and barely breathing, others fidgeting nervously. William glanced at Zerski who, apparently unable to keep his hands still, was rapidly zipping and unzipping his pockets. His jowly face was pinker than usual and covered with droplets of perspiration.

He recognized a few of the officers from the bridge, most of them alert and motionless, as if ready to jump into action should trouble develop. He saw his parents, his father looking stiff and uncomfortable in his high-collared coveralls, his mother twisting a limp handkerchief in her damp hands.

"Murdock, we're ready now," called Captain Stone, from behind him.

"Coming." He turned and made his way to one of the acceleration couches.

"You know how to operate the hands, don't you?" asked the captain.

"Yes, sir, but—"

"None of that, Murdock. It's an honor you've a right to. Inject the water."

"Yes, sir!" William cried, grinning. He patted Starnight's hilt, then took hold of the controls.

Slowly, he made the hands pick up the syringe of water. Then, holding his breath, he maneuvered the needle into the mouth of the container and forced the plunger down.

Nothing happened.

His heart pounded wildly. It *had* to work. It *had* to. "Orion—Cygnus. Help me!" he whispered, staring out past the container to the hard, cold stars. He closed his eyes and hoped.

Suddenly he felt Captain Stone's hand tighten on his arm and from the other room a frantic cheering arose. "It's gone! It's gone! The whole thing disappeared!" shouted the captain.

In the place where the lead container had stood there was nothing.

An instant later, the ship's intercom exploded with a jubilant voice. "I see it! I see it! Earth II! I see it!"

The ship began to rock with the hysterical cheers of two hundred joyous colonists. The hatch flew open. "Billy, my boy! Billy! We knew you could do it," William heard someone call. It was Councilman Zerski, squeezing his way through the small hatch.

Laughing, William threw off his straps and grabbed his crutches. "Excuse me, Mr. Zerski," he said as he pushed past, out into the other chamber. "Come on, Maggie!" he yelled, seizing her by the hand. "Let's go!"

Maggie shrieked with laughter. They catapulted down the shadowy corridor as fast as William could go in his cast. Behind them, the hard walls, usually so silent, rang with voices.

"Come on!" cried Maggie. "Faster! Faster!"

Her breathless laughter came bubbling like water from a well beside him.

Together they tore open the hatch of the observation cone and tumbled through it.

They stopped themselves on the circular walls and hung in the darkness, gasping for breath. "There it is, William," panted Maggie. "Beautiful . . . beautiful . . ."

William's heart almost burst with joy as he gazed through the crystal dome. A jewel in a black velvet case, Earth II hung like a wonderful, gleaming marble before them. And somehow, he knew all would be well. He already imagined the ferry boats bearing the colonists down through that faintly emerald air to a real home at last.

"Home!" he cried. He pulled Starnight smoothly from its sheath and held it up before him. He stared fiercely into the darkness. "Wherever you are," he whispered, "thank you. Thank you."

"Yes," echoed Maggie. "Thank you."

And from somewhere in the brilliant band of stars that seemed to lie thick as dandelions in a meadow beyond their shining planet came an answer—a wave of deep, hearty laughter, and then, *Thank you, little lion!*